The NighT Guardian Book 4 – the Slender Hand of a Blade Smith

Description

In this fantasy story Pendal moves to quickly to consolidate her power and protect her family as guided by her Guardian Angels. As the Dekar-na Empress, the Empress to be, she retains her place out in the world, she is no cloistered pampered female waiting to ascend the throne. Callar her eldest half-brother is dead, executed for his crimes against her but his spirit speaks to her, guiding her to bring her slender hand of justice, a Blade Smith's justice, to a small village called Pletke and uncover new plots by the Emperor against her. This is book four in the NighT Guardian Series, click on the link to purchase and immerse yourself in the adventure.

ISBN Number: 978-1-988441-22-1

Pendal sat by a large elegant window.

Day Rise light streamed in through filtered glass which removed the bright intensity of the suns and allowed just a little of the heat to come through and warm her as she stretched bare legs out on a foot comforter. Although the sun was bright and required filtering, there would not be many more like it. The VodaKhan regions were rapidly moving in toward the season when they would be in the grip of cold, snow, and ice.

She was relaxed, tired, but relaxed.

It was already Mid Day Rise and she had not finished breakfast. The Master of Kitchens had perfected the breakfast she had first purchased on the transport. He had been very unhappy that someone of such stature ate "peasant food" as he called it, but Pendal had been silent and simply stared at him until he had given in and worked with her to get the recipe exactly right. He was also shocked, there was no other word for it, when he found out how spicy she liked her food. Pendal had allowed him to win that battle by agreeing the spices she liked so much would be prepared and presented in separate bowls for her to mix and apply as she desired, not baked into the food.

For once she was sitting on cushions, thin ones with all but a fraction of the stuffing removed, she could still feel the comforting hard boards of the chair under the cushions. But even so, she felt ashamed to be sitting on cushions! Even these that had been especially made for her, the designer had presented two sets to her and had taken the other set away complaining that what he was leaving was nothing more than two pieces of fabric stitched together with nothing between.

Everyone told her yesterday was a special day. It had been the opening of the VodaKhan senate and she had been revealed as the Dekar-na Empress, the Empress to be, the Empress in Waiting, the Empress who would remove the Emperor and restore stability and bring change. Good change, changes that would make people happy both here in VodaKhan and in the southern regions.

After the opening there had been a huge reception, surrounded by Oskar, The High Protector and her mother, Pendal had acknowledged many of those at the opening, people who would actually sit in the Senate, vote and make laws. Her perfect memory remembered every face and every name, every rank and every house or guild the person professed to belong to.

That perfect memory could recount in detail not just the people she met last night, but right back to when she started to remember. The one thing that stood out in all the people, places, and events she had experienced was the first herb she had planted. She could recall every Moon Rise the herb had been in the ground soil and the attention, or not, it required to grow. Every Moon Rise of the herb's life was there clearly in her memory and then she had plucked it from the ground soil and put it with the others to be dried and ground into a fine powder and used with food.

She had been five cycles old, or there abouts when she had planted that first herb and watched it grow, she could remember every other herb she had planted and watched grow since then.

She had left the reception early with the others and retired to a private room for a wonderful meal provided by the Master of Kitchens who managed to keep her food adequately spicy and the others bland. He and his staff had been brought in to the Senate kitchens especially for this occasion. A select number of people from the military, great families, and trade groups sat with them in a warm relaxed atmosphere that never the less spoke to the prideful politics of who and who did not attend a private dinner with the Dekar-na Empress after the opening of the Senate.

Pendal had enjoyed the occasion but ate sparingly; he mind was on Third Moon Rise.

As the dinner came to an end she was the one that hurried Oskar, The High Protector and her mother from the Senate buildings and home.

This Moon Rise was the last when the pre-winter plantings could go into the ground soil.

The herbs would grow through the first cold of winter and would be fresh, cold and tasty when the snow finally covered them. That was the best time to eat them raw, straight from the ground soil, out in the plantings under Moon Rise. Well, that is what she would be doing, the others, they would be inside sleeping and the next day have the herbs served with a warm meal.

Eating raw winter herbs straight from the ground soil was one bad habit Pendal hoped she would never loose.

Oskar, the High Protector and her mother had stood to one side of the plantings and talked of strategy, recounted the events of the day, and discussed who she had met as they watched her down on her knees digging with her hands the holes into which she placed the herbs. As she planted she gave thanks for the strength of the young herbs; she pressed the ground soil around them and carried the heavy casks of river liquid to feed them and help their roots go deep.

As she walked back and forth completing her planting tasks she would stop and join in the conversation, she would add a nuance here and there and with startling clarity she would tell the High Protector and Oskar who was aligned with the Emperor and who was not. These were not disaffected nobles or trade groups, it was rather individuals who saw in the Emperor a way to separate and differentiate their existence and ambitions from those of the group they felt obligated by birth or business to be associated with. But as Pendal pointed out, life for them was good in VodaKhan; they had the luxury of taking their position or dabbling in something risky to spice up their otherwise predictable lives.

Then there was Callar, during the proceedings he had been executed for his crimes.

Pendal did not feel the loss and did not feel the parting of his spirit from the physical plain. His ending when and where it was to take place had been discussed briefly amongst themselves and not allowed to become open knowledge among those who owed allegiance to the Emperor.

Pendal idly took her back blade from its sheath lying on her lap and started to perfect the cleaning of the ground soil from under her nails. She examined the blade in great detail. From the tip of the handle to the tip of the blade, on every side and from every angle, she compared what she saw to what was in her perfect memory of performing the same inspection the day before and the day before that. There was no change. She slipped it back in its sheath and heard the ever so feint hiss of the stone the NighT Guardian had placed in the sheath sharpen the blade as it was replaced. Pendal then removed from its sheath the blade that was constantly on display, the one that sat on her stomach. She heard the same feint hiss of the edge being sharpened. She did not use this one on her nails, but it was examined with the same minute detail. The throwing blades in her boots had been examined in detail before breakfast had been brought in. Last, but not forgotten, the blade in her pack had been taken out and examined as well.

The blades were examined in this way every day and after every use.

No Illusions

Pendal was under no delusion.

These blades and her skills with them were life giving. Also life giving was her body armour, sitting relaxed, with bare legs in the Mid Day Rise glow of the window she was never the less wearing her torso armour under her relaxed robes.

There was a knock at the door, the guards outside would announce the visitor if it were not one of a few that had immediate access such as her mother, Oskar or the High Protector. As the door opened without an announcement, Pendal knew it was one of those three.

It was Oskar.

He came over to the window and Pendal beckoned him to sit in the chair facing her. As he sat, Pendal put her feet down and sat more upright. He looked at her with some mild concern. "Even in this fortress, I hope you are…" Pendal stopped him completing his sentence by tapping her chest with the spoon from her breakfast bowl. The sound of it on her torso armour was distinctive even though muffled by the robes she was wearing. Oskar nodded that he approved.

"Callar, before he was executed gave up several more high level Imperial agents; members of a trading guild, and two great families aligned with the same guild. There was also the matter of a shipping and transport operation, all perfectly legal but some of its operatives were smuggling gold out of VodaKhan for their own benefit."

Pendal looked at him, he looked both more energized than when they first met and tired at the same time. "What's the matter?" She asked.

It took a while for Oskar to respond. "We have been lazy and overly confident." He sighed as he said the last word and looked out of the window at the gardens below. "We control the volume and frequency of the gold shipments sent to the Imperial family. Those shipments have kept them in power and allowed us direct influence. We have the ability to guide the Imperial senate through a combination of our senators and the lesser ones who follow our instructions." He paused again and looked the birds flying past the window as they chased insects stirred up from the clearing away of old dead plants. "Have you ever had an interest in the flowering plants? Like the ones in the garden below?" He asked.

Oskar looked sideways at Pendal for a response, perhaps a way to divert her attention from the deficiencies he was admitting to. "For a long time, we have seen the military campaigns of the Emperor as his way of trying to influence events, turn the other great families to his side and against us. We have been very effective in making his adventures come to naught and to make his situation worse." Oskar stopped and sat back into the deep cushions of his chair.

Pendal adjusted her blade belt on her lap, "While you were watching the Emperors hand guide his legions back and forwards across the southern regions you were not looking at his other hand here in VodaKhan." She took her main blade out of its sheath and held it in the sun light between them, using its highly polished blackness to reflect the light across the floor and walls of the room and finally let it settle its reflection on Oskar's hands resting on his stick.

Oskar stared at the bright-reflected light on his hands for some time but it was Pendal who continued to speak. "The fact is you were thinking of, looking for, and prepared for a web of sophisticated Imperial spies yet what you are finding are a few high-level spies like Callar but they are using simple thieves, robbers and murderers." Pendal paused, "and you are finding greed and desire among some members of Great and Minor houses and in trade groups. Probably they were just people who felt it made them important or they were bored or could not see their lives improving any other way." She put away her blade and watched as Oskar sat further well back in the thick cushions and made extra room for himself by wriggling his torso and head.

He closed his eyes.

Pendal thought Oskar was going to take a nap or even sleep but the sharp intake of breath through his teeth assured her otherwise. "How do you do it?" He asked with his eyes still closed.

Pendal was taken slightly off guard by the question, "what do you mean, how do I do it? Do what?" She asked.

"Sum it up so neatly," he said and paused, "I suppose you are going to say it all comes from growing up in that monetary!"

Pendal made a slight smile and responded, "Yes, I am. But not quite as you think." She stopped to organize her thoughts before continuing. "It was serving in the hospital, tending sick, injured and dying members of the order, locals and travelers." She let out a long slow breath and looked out the window at the gardeners working at making the pretty flowering plants look extra special and appropriate to the changing seasons. The herb plantings were her domain, the gardeners would never touch them, and, they would never be allowed to touch them, she had made that clear. "There were always some who I cared for that would be seriously ill, and some would come to the monastery just so their spirits could pass over to the next world in a place of peace, quiet and caring. Part of my duties was to give observance to their passing." She paused. "In that time when they came to know there was no hope of remaining in the physical world, we would observe their life, their secrets, what had brought them pleasure, what had brought them sadness. What they had done that was wrong, and why they felt doing bad things was justified. The things they had not done that they should have." She paused, it was hard to keep the door to that part of her perfect memory closed. The door was heavy and strong, like a door set in a castle wall and she had become expert at keeping it closed, on the other side was an army of memories of the people she had given observance to as they passed over. Those memories longed to live again if only for a moment and tried desperately to open the door just a crack and slip through.

Pendal redoubled her efforts at keeping the door closed, and slamming it with a mental fist to tell those memories o the other side that it was worthless to keep trying to open the door. But it sent the army of memories into a frenzy trying every which way to open the door before eventually quieting down.

Silence sat in the third chair at the window and waited.

Oskar opened his eyes slowly and looked at Pendal, she was in deep thought and concentration and staring down at her blade belt. "I never knew. How many cycles where you when you started giving observance?"

Pendal had some memories, behind another door that she felt safe to open and she would let a selected memory here and there come out into the light and live again for a short while. She opened that door and an old man stooped over from working in the plantings came out and looked around, he looked up at the sun through Pendal's eyes and he waved to Pendal as she watched him in her minds eye. The seasons around him changed quickly, he had been to the monastery several times for treatment of illness and she remembered him from each visit; from standing and waving to her, she soon saw him in a cot and very ill. Some friends brought him to the monastery that last time and went back to his home to divide up and take away his possessions.

They knew he would not be returning.

"I am not sure, I don't even know how many cycles I am…." She paused, she did not dwell on her age. "The first person I gave observance to was an old man, a local, he was very ill, he was nearly one hundred and twenty cycles; as I count my cycles I was ten cycles, maybe eleven. He had been married all his life and had a family, his spouse had died many cycles before and the children had moved away, he had lived alone for the last part of his life, until he became too ill and was brought to us. What he most wanted observed before he passed was his regret at not doing what he wanted to do, but especially when he chose his spouse." Pendal stopped, and looked at the chair where silence sat and then back at Oskar and out of the window at the gardeners who were taking a break and drinking river liquid and eating their packaged food. "He had a love when he was young, they loved each other deeply and planed to become spouses, have a family and take some land and start working it. But his parents persuaded him to choose another for his spouse."

Pendal stopped and looked at the memory of the old man lying in the cot, in the corner of the room at the monastery hospital, from which he would never leave alive. "His first love had begged him to be his own person and not allow himself to be persuaded to chose another. But his parents prevailed and his first love was lost. He loved the woman he married but never quite as much as the first love of his life. And, for the rest of his life it seemed he was never quite doing what he wanted to do," She paused.

"He was always being persuaded to do something he was not quite happy with, the results were never bad, but his burden was that he always felt things could be better, easier, happier if he did what he wanted to do the way he wanted it. He wished he had the strength not to allow others to make decisions for him." Pendal let out a long breath.

"He felt his life was a series of regrets, that after every time he did what someone else wanted he promised himself he would do what he wanted the next time. When the next time arrived, he did not have the courage to stand for himself and others told him what to do."

"I told him this time he would make his own decision on when to pass over, I would hold his hand and feel his spirit leave his body but I would not make the decision for him."

Silence in the third chair leaned forward and put its arms around Pendal and Oskar for several moments.

"After I told him that he smiled and thanked me and passed over very quickly. It was shortly after that I felt a warm hug and a hand stroke my face." Pendal stopped talking and looked out of the window.

"You were ten cycles when that happened... I never knew what the monastery could ask of someone so young...." Oskar said quietly, not completing his sentence.

"I might have been eleven...." Said Pendal.

"Maybe eleven..." said Oskar. "But, an adult."

Pendal let out a deep sigh, "No, not an adult, a girl of ten or eleven cycles. I knew no different, I thought all girls, and some boys at the monastery of that age gave observance at someone's passing."

Silence sat back in the deep cushions of the third chair, there would be no more words for some time, and it was happy.

Eyes Open

Pendal woke up.

Her senses were fully awake, her eyes were closed. Her slender hand had never let go of the blade handle lying on her lap but now it tightened with the strength of a reptile in the southern regions that killed by crushing the life out of its prey. Her feet moved and planted themselves squarely on the floor.

As the NighT Guardian taught her before she left, she made no other movements and her breathing did not change, her heart rate that raced for a moment was now slowed and beating at the normal pace of when she was sleeping.

Silence still sat attentively in the third chair by the window, watching, waiting for it knew it would be gone soon.

Across from Pendal, Oskar's breathing was that of a person in deep sleep.

Pendal rolled her head in the way a person roils their head when they are dreaming, it was a slow and relaxed movement but her position now gave her a better view of the door and she opened her eyes a fraction so she could see any potential threats that might have come in, somehow, past the guards.

Nothing.

Bracing her feet and holding the belt with its sheath for her back blade she stood, carefully. In the third chair silence watched her move like river liquid flowing over rocks that is at once clear like a looking glass, but is yet deep and powerful. Bare footed Pendal moved from room to room conducting a search using her eyes, her ears and with the help of her guardian spirits for anything that might be out of place. As she moved, she attached her belt and tested the position of her blades front and back. They were in ideal position for her hands.

In the planning room, sitting at the head of the large table around which they sat and planned and learned about the ways and methods of the Imperial Spies was a shadowy figure. Half there, half not, but a little more sometimes than others.

Callar.

His spirit… had returned.

Pendal understood the need for some spirits to communicate after their passing; they needed to converse with the physical world one last time for some reason. They had a message. In her mind she heard some simple words, "I am happy now… It is over… It was not what I wanted… I had to do it… Save the family." Callar turned to look at her; it was a happy face, a relaxed face. One hand rested on a map, his finger pointed to a location on it. She walked around the back of the chair the apparition was sitting in; as she did she looked over at the map to where its finger was pointing.

Callar's image faded, the last of the image to disappear were his hands one appeared to hold the edge of the table while the other had never moved from the location it pointed to.

Pendal moved around the table so she was facing the door, as she did she turned the map so it was the right way for her look at it. She bent over placing both fists on the table for support and concentrated on the location Callar was pointing at.

"Pletke" she said slowly and quietly, it was the name of the place Callar's finger had been resting on. Pendal was not sure what it meant, but his arm stretched awkwardly to allow his finger to rest on it so there must be some reason for it. She took a writing instrument from the table and drew a circle around it.

At the door to the room there was the rustling of clothes. "I am sorry, I fell asleep," said Oskar.

"I fell asleep to, I think we both needed it," replied Pendal. She rotated the map so that Oskar could see the circle she had drawn. He moved over to the table and looked down at the map.

"Pletke," he rolled the word around in his mouth, saying it several times with different emphasis on the letters in the name. Finally, he looked up, "I have never heard of the place, I have no idea what is there. Why is it important?" He asked.

Pendal did not describe quite what happened; Oskar was open to many things, but they were all physical, it would take some time to mentor him to understand there was more to the world than what he could touch with his hand. All that was important was that he trusted her.

"And," said Pendal, "we must save my family, the NighT Guardian, my brother and sisters, and Cavahn. Bringing them to VodaKhan would be the safest for them," she said as she straightened herself up from looking over the table.

Close to Pletke

Day Rise had not started, Pendal's mind was with her father in his watchtower, looking up at the sky lights twinkling next to the moons, and the moon's light reflecting off the river Ohm switching this way and that back and forth across the valley floor. Now was about right for the change of guardianship, when the NighT Guardians gave their duties to the Day Guardians and left to go home, for her father to retire to the beautiful house down by the River Ohm.

The horse she was riding, the same one she rode to the route stop where she had first met Callar, suddenly halted.

His action brought Pendal's focused mind back to the present.

The thick reeds next to the river to her left were swaying back and forth in the mild breeze, the river here, ran quicker than further up where she had joined the trail. Ahead though the reeds were not swaying they seemed to be in a whirlwind of disruption, back and forth and in complete difference to the rest of the reeds around them, curse words were coming from the disruption. Pendal took in the clean smell of the river and the cool crisp pre-winter air that seemed to clean her nose of all other smells she had smelt for the past few days.

She waited for the disruption to clear itself. As she waited the disruption of the reeds stopped. It was replaced by splashing and more curse words. With a loud curse word, a man came out of the reeds, over his shoulder a large sack wriggling violently. From it came various grunts, slaps and small bellowing sounds like a feed animal would make just after it came out of its mother womb and was dropped on the floor.

The man had been catching river creatures and had quite the catch; Pendal thought he had perhaps six or seven in the sack. Taken from the river liquid the man had not killed them before putting them in the sack, now they were thrashing brutally against each other as they died, the violence would break them, releasing their blood and breaking up their flesh. Rather than have six or seven creatures to eat or sell, he would have perhaps half that number by the time all were dead.

The man saw Pendal and froze. She sensed he felt guilty, she was not sure of what. There was no restriction on catching river creatures, perhaps he felt guilty at the way he was transporting them, of the waste of their lives, their bodies, and flesh.

"Priest, I thank you for the bounty you have blessed me with," he said.

Pendal looked at the man, he was maybe a head less tall than the NighT Guardian and quite thin, his clothes fitted where they touched his body. He was not wearing boots, then Pendal saw them and a scything blade used for working in the fields cutting down crops, this man was a harvester. Groups of men with scything blades would arrange themselves in a long line and then sweep across a field of plantings cutting them down to be gathered and processed into food. On the other side of the road well away from the river, the boots were in no danger of ending up wet or in the river, he could not wear wet boots in a field of plantings and without a scything blade, he was not a harvester.

"I have not provided you with bounty. Not killing the river creatures before putting them in the sack allows them to thrash against each other as they die releasing their blood and damaging their flesh, you will have only a few left you can eat. I have not blessed you, I do not bless stupid people," she said. The man turned away from Pendal, and appeared to fix his gaze on his boots and scything blade.

Pendal, turned too look at a cart behind it her. It was a covered cart, four large wheels and four stout, strong horses pulled it. The driver sat inside a covered arch and gave Pendal a small hand signal, which she returned equally carefully. The cart rolled past Pendal and for a moment the flap at he back was held open by a strong hand and a very intent face looked at her, then the flap was closed. Part of her guard detail. Across the field to her right, she could make out the partial shape of a rider surveying the scene, another part of her guard detail.

The man looked at the cart as it made its way along the road, the thrashing in his sack had almost ended, perhaps just one river creature left alive and making its final struggles before it died.

"I know!" The man said. "It is not that I am a bad person; I do not enjoy it when the creatures struggle so and die. You see the other harvesters in my band are old men, they do not have many teeth left with which to bite and chew." He looked up at Pendal. "The trashing of the creatures and their bleeding out softens the flesh so they can eat it with their gums."

As he spoke, Pendal could see that he too did not have many teeth at the front of his mouth. Pendal raised her left hand with the its palm facing the man she drew a sacred symbol in the air, "you are blessed for what you do for your band." She said.

The man looked at her for a moment as if deciding whether to say something or not, then he opened his mouth, "Priest, I do not recognize the symbol with which you blessed me, what order are you from? He asked.

Pendal considered the man for a moment; it was the correct question to ask, receiving a blessing from a priest using a symbol you do not know is important. "I am a priest from the order of Garfan," said Pendal.

The man's eyes opened wider than they had been, as did his mouth at the same time. "We had a priest from that order when I was very young, when just starting as a harvester. She was encouraging and mindful of us even though we were just harvesters. I enjoyed my time in her company, I was very sad when she left. Since then we have only had grey priests that are harsh, task masters, they fill us with obligations and duties we must perform." He said.

He bowed his head as Pendal rode by.

Pletke

Pendal stood beside her horse, a handful of grains in her hand, which he was eating. Pletke was ahead of her, the river where she had met the harvester had always been and still was on her left. A ridge and trees hid another part of her guard detail. The cart that held those closest to her sat to one side of the road close to the sign that announced the village's name. All around were bare fields; the harvesters had cleared them in time for the cooler nights leading into winter which would kill any of the feed plantings left out.

All three moons had set, this was the magical time when the moons were gone and Day Rise had not begun, Pendal always loved this time the most. It seemed the most magical and quiet.

She had been watching a small boat cross the river and leave three people on the far side, there had been an exchange of disks and the boat was on its way back. On the far side, there was a building with fenced in land that came down to the rivers edge. Horses moved freely inside the fence and also went in to and came out of the building without restriction. The people left on the far side had paid for horses, saddles and other riding equipment.

Pendal's horse looked where Pendal was looking and shook its head violently and stomped its front feet. Pendal sensed from its spirit one emotion, "betrayal." Pendal scratched the horse's nose and thanked its spirit. "That old trick she said as she looked into its eyes. Thank you, it had not occurred to me." She said.

The driver from the cart with part of her guard detail came up to her and patted her horse, it looked to an observer as if they were two travelers who had stopped by the side of the road talking. "Why have we stopped he asked?"

Pendal studied the square jawed soldier for a long moment. "Before entering Pletke, I thought I would find out what sort of a place it was." She said.

He looked at her, "How can you tell that from here? We could enter the village and search it, we have the right." He said.

"No, said Pendal we will learn all we need to very shortly." She nodded to the river and the boat which was just a short distance from where it docked. She told him what had taken place, how the boat had delivered three to the other side for a fee and how those travelers had arranged horses and riding equipment from the building on the other side. He looked and listened but seemed as if he were doing it to humor Pendal.

All of a sudden there was shouting and the pounding of hooves from the trail that led up and over a small ridge and into trees and thick bushes behind the building. Suddenly two horses, without riders rather playfully came over the ridge and trotted into the building and out into the fenced in area. Two men came from the house to catch the horses and quickly remove their saddles.

The third horse came over the hill much slower as it's rider still had his foot trapped in his foot harness and was being dragged on his back, he was shouting loudly and waving his arms trying to get the horse's attention and make it stop. The men who removed the other saddles left them where they were and came rushing out to the road. One stood in front of the horse, which was slowing down and caught its head harness and stopped it from going any further, the other went to man on the ground who was thanking both of them for their help and mercy at stopping the runaway horse. Rather than help the man on the ground, his rescuer knelt on his chest and took out a blade and slashed the man's throat. There was silence.

Over the ridge came two men walking beside a horse. On each side of the horse, it pulled two bodies tied to the saddle by long ropes. With all the three bodies together they set about robbing the corpses and stripping them of clothing, then they took the bodies to the edge of the river and eased them in to the liquid. As they walked back up to the buildings, they patted each other on the back.

The soldier turned to Pendal and closed his mouth slowly, "I see," he said.

Pendal looked at him, "we have learned a lot about Pletke in a very short time," she said. She scratched the nose of her horse, "I have seen this before. Somewhere on the road over the ridge and out of site there is a marker, the horses are trained to throw their riders at that point. Robbers are hiding in the trees and bushes; they kill and rob the fallen riders. The rest you have seen. As to the harvester, yes, I learned the priest in Pletke is a bitch; I will deal with her" said Pendal firmly.

A small crowd gathers

Even though it was still early a small crowd had gathered.

Pendal sat at a corner table of a small eating-place sipping at spiced root juice.

In the middle of the village square a stature of the village's founder stood on top of a fountain decorated with river creatures from whose mouths poured appropriately, river liquid, chains hung in short intervals from the rim of the fountain. There was nothing on the end of the chains, the cups that had been attached and allowed people to drink freely had been cut off and stacked in a cage. An old harvester to infirm to go to the fields guarded the cage and gave out the cups in return for some low value disks. He explained to Pendal that he gathered up the cups after they had been used for a drink, if more than one cup of liquid was wanted, more disks had to be handed over. It was not his idea he stressed, it was the grey priest and all disks had to be handed over to her.

Pendal on hearing this had over turned the cage, broken it and picked a cup and drank several times from the fountain liquid as the old man protested.

Pendal had taken from her purse several high value disks and placed them in the old man's hand and told him to leave. He first looked at the disks in his hand and then at her with an expression of complete amazement, "This is more disk than I have earned in my entire life, this will take to my end in great comfort, are you sure I do not have to give it over to the priest?" He looked down at the disks and then up at Pendal again, "would you…?" His hand closed around the disks, he looked intently in to Pendal's eyes, "Would you observe my passing?"

Pendal looked at the old man, everything in her told her he had many more cycles before she would have to observe his passing. "Yes, I will observe your passing but I think you have many cycles left," she reached out and touched the old man's face. As she did he stood shakily, and put the disks away in the folds of his clothes.

"What shall I tell the priest about this…" he waved his arm at the broken cage and cups on the ground and at the bottom of the fountain liquid.

Pendal instead asked the old man a question of faith, "Do you believe in judgment?" She asked. The old man stopped for a moment, thinking it a trick question and then said that he did, as there was no other answer possible. Pendal turned to him and instructed him to tell the priest that she was here to create judgment, and the judge should not be kept waiting.

She also told the old man to tell as many as were awake and about the village and what would be happening. They were welcome to come and witness the judgment of the grey priest. Pendal could see at the corner of the square, a group of old harvesters who had shambled in and one that was not quite so old carrying a sack over his shoulder dripping blood. Pendal pointed to them, and the old man smiled a toothless grin. He told her they were his friends and it looked like they would have the flesh of river creatures to fill their empty bellies today. Pendal told him she knew, she had seen the younger man by the side of the river and had blessed him.

She had asked him why his belly was empty, it was the duty of the priest to ensure the poor and infirm such as he were taken care of and loved by the whole village. His reply was that this was not the way of the priest who would not allow food or any other comfort to be given to the poor.

The old man had asked for a blessing but before he received it, he reached back into his clothing and pulled out one of the high value disks Pendal had just given him. He told her he must pay for the blessing and that she should take back the disk. But Pendal sternly told him blessing were free and had took more high value disks out and pressed them into his shaking hand. He had nodded when she asked if the priest had set payment for blessings.

As the old man shuffled off to the other harvesters, Pendal strode back to her table, as she did she heard several taps of approval from a stick against the tiled floor of the eating-place. Pendal did not look at Oskar.

As the number of people grew in the village square, Pendal sipped a little deeper on her root juice. She had to admit the eating-place made good root juice. A slightly older man came to her table than their server with more spices with a fresh pot of steaming juice. He looked at the empty pots and stopped pouring, "So much spice and heat, I have never seen anyone use that much," he said as he started to pour again. He looked Pendal in the eyes as he spoke, "You must not do this, she is the priest of the village, and she has been for many cycles. She is hard, an outsider would say things are wrong here but belief is belief, and she has guided us in it in all spiritual ways." He stopped speaking and stopped pouring juice into Pendal's bowl. "There have been other priests. They have come and seen what they believe to be wrong and decided to give judgment…" He started to nervously start pouring; as he did he started speaking again, "… they are in the river. Please do not tell anyone I spoke of this," he looked Pendal in the eyes, "If you survive that is." He bowed and moved back inside quickly.

Pendal said nothing.

The message had been sent to the priest that she was to be judged under the sky, under the sky so that all who wished to be present could see; this would not be a closed judgment. It would start at the time between when Moonrise ended and Day Rise had not started.

Pendal had only ever seen one priest judged, the priest was deranged after spending most of her life in a mountain prayer retreat but had still made a good case for continuing as priest of the retreat. But there had been too many errors and false rules of belief, strange happenings that could not be ignored. The priest was removed and cared for to the end of her days, which had come soon after judgment.

The harvester she had seen on the road appeared in front of her. He held out his right hand in it were a few small value disks, Pendal saw the inside of his forearm which was marked with lines that clearly had been put there by a burning iron of some sort. He bowed to Pendal.

"You blessed me at the side of the road. You did not collect your duty," he said quietly.

Pendal still looking at the markings on his forearm asked how he came by them. The harvester explained that the priest had burned his arm with a special penance iron she had, she would burn the arms of people who had received blessings but had insufficient disks to pay for them. Sufficient disks had to be produced by the time the burning healed, if the disks were not forthcoming, the priest would not observe the person's passing. Pendal placed a high value disk in his hand and closed his hand around all the disks and told him to leave, when the time came, as with his friend, she would be there to observe his passing.

The harvester stood there for a long moment trying to take in what Pendal had said and the value of the disk Pendal had pressed into his hand.

Pendal could sense the priest's coming; there was a change in the small crowd, they had been talking quietly amongst themselves until now. Now they were silent, and a little nervous. The first pale glimmer of Day Rise was starting to spread in the sky from the west. Pendal shrugged off her cloak and set it aside. Her priestly attire, the black collar with its sacred symbols was now visible to all.

The Grey Priest

....Appeared.

Suddenly.

The harvester standing in front of Pendal had hidden her arrival. She had been remarkably quiet in her movements.

The priest reached out and pulled the harvester's hair at the back jerking his head back and screamed in his face that he must leave. The man bowed begging forgiveness and shuffled away quickly.

The priest's robes were grey; different parts of her clothing had different shades of grey. There was no collar, but from around her neck hung several golden symbols on heavy gold chains. At the back of her neck the chains disappeared in folds of skin that were also grey. Her hair was sparse and grey and where there was no hair there was grey coloured, wrinkled, skin. She was similar to Pendal in height but thinner and much older. The woman did have a full set of teeth Pendal noted but the front teeth at the top and bottom had been filed to points that when they closed interlocked like saw blades. It was a tradition Pendal had heard of at the monastery, it was intended to represent the gates at the entrance to the mines where souls of non-believers and wrong doers would toil for many life times until their broken spirits were allowed back to the surface. Using the sharpened teeth, the priest would bite into still bloodied meat and tear out a piece to symbolize a soul being dragged bloodied down into the mines. Some wild rumors said there were priests who had become deranged would bite into a person they decided was a wrong doer and take a piece of flesh from the person as an example to the others.

Pendal set aside the bowl of root juice and slowly stood, as she did she spoke to her guides asking they be with her and guide her in her actions in all ways of the judgment.

The way in which Pendal carried out the simple act of rising from sitting at a table made the grey priest stand back a pace of two. Pendal appeared to glide from one position to the next with the ease of someone who is so totally on the present that no effort is required.

As Pendal stepped out into the first rays of Day Rise the light caught the sacred symbols on her black collar and they appeared to glow with intensity far greater than simple light striking gold on a black background.

The grey priest slightly lowered her face so that her eyes looked out from under her eyebrows and Pendal saw more of the grey skin that covered the forehead into the thinning hairline. The grey priest flexed her fingers as if preparing to grapple. Pendal looked at her fingernails, they too had been filed to points but were blackened and dirty, and some of the nails were broken and not repaired. Pendal would not grapple with this grey priest. Infection from a cut with those nails or a bite from those teeth was highly probable. As the grey priest took half a pace to the left, and then back, and half a pace to the right, she was intently staring at the sacred symbols on Pendal's collar, she was trying to read them, as she moved she hissed at Pendal until spit started to run down her chin on to the stained front of her robe.

Although the grey priest appeared to keep her distance, she did so not knowing Pendal's abilities; she was still well within Pendal's striking range.

"I see!" She exclaimed loudly, pointing at Pendal, the shout was for the benefit of the small gathering, "Symbols from Garfan Order!" She stopped and turned her back to Pendal and walked over to the fountain, as she did she kicked some of the cups spilled on the floor. Then she returned to face Pendal but this time she was further away fidgeting on her feet. "I see!" She exclaimed loudly, "Symbols from the Order of 1!"

"This priest is not pure… She is from two orders! She wears other symbols that mean nothing!" Shrieked the grey priest to the small gathering. "I will do as I have done to the others who have come to judge their better! I will send them to the mines by eating of their impure flesh to save us all!" The grey priest started to move further right and left but Pendal did not move, she would not be encouraged to leave the bright First Day Rise light.

The ground where the grey priest was trying to get Pendal to move to was uneven and had been whetted by spillage of liquid from the fountain.

Pendal was happy on the level ground in front of the eating-place but she was also happy on uneven ground, even whetted ground, but she would not move in the direction the grey priest wanted, the grey priest expected her to move to the left and deeper into shadow so that Pendal would be looking up and in to the Day Rise light reflected off a white painted wall of a nearby building.

Pendal was in control.

To Pendal's right, even brighter more pure rays of Day Rise not filtered by trees and houses, and not reflecting off buildings was striking the ground. Pendal moved to the right, and stood in the bright clear rays of First Day Rise.

The sacred symbols on her collar exploded in the brightness and looked as if a great deity had painted them. The maroon of her priestly robes edged with blue and gold shimmered now. Although Pendal's heavy boots grounded her effortlessly, her appearance suddenly in the brighter light seemed to be magical like a spirit gliding from one place that was bright into anther place of intense brightness.

But the grey priest was also suddenly a great deal closer to Pendal than she expected or wanted to be and it was she who was in the long shadow cast by one of the buildings.

The grey priest swung her left arm in Pendal's direction with the fingers held straight and rigid making the broken nails on her fingers a cutting edge, it was a crude movement and Pendal easily avoided it.

"You would cut the one who is here to judge you?" Pendal said in an even, level, tone that carried to the corners of the square.

"You cannot judge me, I cannot be judged, I give order, and balance, and I punish. My order is strong because of me and I am strong because of my order. The strong remain strong and the weak and poor remain slaves," howled Pendal's opponent.

"And those who take the ferry across and are murdered? Asked Pendal.

"They pay for blessings before they cross and then they give up their wealth for my order on the other side," she said. As she spoke another crude move to attack Pendal started, again with her left hand. She had missed before and now she tried bringing her arm over her shoulder and lunged at Pendal in an effort to bring the black stained sharpened nails down on Pendal's face.

Pendal, still in the bright rays of light lifted her right fist to meet the wrist of the grey priest's arm descending on her. The wrist of the grey priest broke as it collided with Pendal's fist.

The grey priest had placed a great deal of her body weight behind the move and Pendal used the arm with its broken wrist as leverage to throw the priest away from her. The grey priest slipped on the uneven ground, as she had intended Pendal to but finally kept her balance. She looked with hatred at Pendal and her hand sticking out from the broken wrist at a strange angle.

Silence now sat in Pendal's chair at her table and watched transfixed. It covered all in the eating-place and in the square.

Pendal had not moved from the bright first rays of Day Rise.

From the hunched over figure of the grey priest came sounds of wild shrieking and cursing, blood appeared on the ground from violent coughing.

Pendal again using her clear level toned voice pronounced her judgment, for all to hear. The grey priest was not caring and nurturing, she was neglect full and tortured and maimed. She was not a bringer of love and healing; the grey priest persecuted and enslaved and kept the poor, poor, she condoned murder and extracted disks for blessings. Blessings Pendal made sure all understood were free. Blessings she said were the simplest and greatest gift that could be given by a priest and received by a penitent. She taught greed and hate were natural and normal instead of abhorrent and detestable. River liquid was free to all, not to bought and sold. The grey priest would be removed and not return. Healing priests from the orders of Garfan and 1 would be sent to heal the village and all whom grey priest had come into contact with.

The grey priest shrieked at the judgment and whirled, still hunched over, her sharpened teeth stained with blood from her coughing she lunged at Pendal with her right hand reaching out and shaped like a claw. Pendal easily side stepped the charge and tapped the woman's ankle hard with her boot, there was a shout of pain and the grey priest moved away limping from the bright pool of light Pendal had made her own. The priest was moving towards a blade dropped by the liquid seller when Pendal had smashed the cage in which the cups had been locked.

Pendal did not want to blade fight this priest, this was a religious judgment being carried out and the grey priest had to be taken to her order. Besides, Pendal could so very easily defeat the woman. She reached down to her boots and took out both throwing blades, as she straightened she arched her back slightly and brought both hands back behind her head and then swiftly forward releasing her slightly arched back as she threw the blades.

Both blades left her hands at great speed and force but for a moment appeared in the golden rays of First Day Rise as darts of a slender and beautiful shape. The blades hit the backs of the grey priests knees pinning her robe to the back of her legs. The grey priest stopped walking and lost interest in the blade on the ground, she pulled up the front of her robe to reveal the point of a throwing blade sticking out from each kneecap.

She screamed and cursed, and tried to turn to reach behind her to take the blades out of her knees but could not reach either of them with her one good hand. As she thrashed around trying to move she fell over and began to cry and scream and twitch like a child.

Soldiers appeared and rushed to retrain the Grey Priest and remove Pendal's throwing blades.

Day Rise was now much fuller stunningly clear. Pendal stood there in bright light and made the symbol of blessing to all in the square.

Behind her the fierce and repeated tapping of Oskar's stick on the cobbled floor of the eating-place was like a drum beat.

Pendal sat and sipped her root juice and looked down at her throwing blades. They had been taken from the grey priest's knees and carefully cleaned by the eating-place owner and laid in front of her on separate clean clothes. Pendal was studying them closely as she did all her other blades every day and after any use, she turned them over one by one, and studied both sides, the handles and the blade edges and then the points. Then one by one she put them back in the sheathes in her boots.

She looked up.

People were surrounding the fountain, looking at the liquid and waiting to take a cup and drink freely from the liquid in the fountain. A metal worker had fashioned additional cups and was attaching them to the chains that had hung from the fountain rim without use for many years.

At the far left of the square the men from the other side of the river who had murdered many and stolen their possessions were in wrist, leg, and neck chains. Added to them now was the civil director of the village. He had the power to stop the grey priest, have her removed, and a new priest sent to the village but he had not. Later he had become an enforcer of her strange behaviour, requests and demands. He had joined with her and devised demands of his own which the Grey Priest pronounced as religious requirements and from which he benefited greatly. VodaKhan soldiers guarded them while they waited for a cart to come and take them away to prison and execution.

To the left of where Pendal and Oskar sat a table had been set up by the owner of the eating-place. Villagers were coming to look at Pendal, some ventured close to thank her for her judgment of the Grey Priest and leave fruit, fresh river creatures, or food items for her. She refused any artifacts; gathering wealth she explained not something she was allowed to do.

Villagers stopped to ask for a personal blessing but there were so many that she had blessed the entire village simply instead.

Oskar had not said anything for some time. He had lived his life in power, and secrecy and with military force all around him. This was the first time he had seen Pendal in action, in a manner of speaking. And he could feel the sense of relief in the villagers, it was thick and tangible as if it could be touched and eaten. It was a revelation to him how the village had changed in such as short time period.

Pendal flexed her shoulders and looked around the village square. She sniffed the air. It was there. Extremely feint but she could smell the snow, cold, and ice that would be coming to the village. She looked around the square. At the far right of her the harvesters were using a flat rock to cut and eat their river creatures raw.

Pendal stood.

She beckoned the owner of the eating-place and pointed to the harvesters and asked why they were eating uncooked food. He explained that the priest had closed the building they used for cooking, washing, and to live in during the cold winter when they could not harvest. Also, it was likely they had not eaten for several days and were starving. He said rather cautiously that since Pendal had arrived there had been great bounty in the river and all around the village.

Pendal directed that he cook their river creatures and add the field crops land other food left for her on the table. Then she asked to be shown the closed harvester's building.

A used stable

The harvester's building had once been a stable for horses. It had been repaired and she could see it was warm and dry. The sleeping stalls for horses had been converted so that one or two harvesters each had a cot to sleep in, and a place to be private and keep their possessions. There was a communal bathing area and kitchen for food preparation.

Pendal, Oskar and two officers were wandering around the space that would accommodate fifteen or twenty harvesters through the winter. Pendal breathed in and breathed out slowly as she walked around and inspected everything. As she inspected, she made a mental list of what was missing. There were no blankets or any sort of warm covering for sleeping and the cots were bare of sleeping pads, while she would be comfortable on the hard wood floor, the old harvesters would not. There were no cups, eating or cooking utensils.

Oskar looked at Pendal, "So what do you think, do you have a long list of what is missing?" He said. The officers stood idly by gazing at this or that. It was far less impressive than what they were used to.

Pendal came out of the showering and personal washing area and looked at the officers, "Tell me, what do you see that is missing here that is also missing at your barracks?" They started back at Pendal and then at each other, then at Oskar who shrugged.

None of them could answer.

Pendal ran her slender fingers along the heavy eating table in front of them, "For a place that has not been used since the Grey Priest arrived, some twenty two cycles ago, there is no dust anywhere, and everything is spotlessly clean. Do you not find that odd?" She asked. "why the need to keep a building that is not used so clean?" She asked.

Suddenly, Oskar started to look around, his eyes widening, "Perhaps she had the place cleaned?" He asked.

"I don't think so," replied Pendal. "To clean a place this size would require more than one person and a number of implements and cleaning liquids. I have not found any, which means they would have to be brought here; the cleaning performed, and then the implements and remaining liquids removed. Why remove them, there are closets for them at one side of the washing area. On the floor there are stains and marks from both implements and liquids." Pendal said.

The sound of the front door being unlatched slowly filled the room. The officers started to draw their blades, Pendal, did not, and even before the door was completely open to allow the person outside to look in, she had waved the officers to put away their blades.

Over the heavy doorstep a bare dirty leg appeared and then the man she had seen catching river creatures followed it. He looked uncertainly at them but then was lost in the space he found inside. He shuffled forward from the door into the main entry way and then into the main room. As he inspected the first sleeping area he looked nervous. He carried his boots and a small bag of possessions.

"If you are looking to decide on where to rest during the winter," said Pendal pausing, "I would choose one further away from the main door, there will be cold air coming in as the door is opened and closed." Said Pendal.

"I have had to sleep outside or under animal feed most of my life because of the Grey Priest, and today I had cooked food because of you. There are no words of gratitude I can speak for what you have done." As he spoke, the door opened again and a much older harvester appeared and was helped over the doorstep by two other equally old but firmer bodied men, he looked at them caringly. "Please, help my father to a cot away from the door," he said to the two helpers of the old man.

He then turned and looked at a cot facing Pendal and placed his boots by the entrance and his small bag of possessions on the floor beside the cot. He held his arms out and shook his hands as if testing the space around the cot, which his arms could not touch. Then he turned and came back to the main table where Pendal, Oskar and the two officers stood.

"I cannot believe I am allowed to stand here, to have so much space that my hands cannot touch the walls.... Or to touch these things" He reached out and touched the large wooden table that Pendal still had her hand on. Then he looked at the Head of Table chair, which was larger and more comfortable than the others, he walked over to it and ran his hand over the back of the chair. Then he patted the chair back and turned to Pendal, "This is where the Emperor sits when he comes to Pletke to hide from his nobles and senate in the south," he said.

Silence was sitting cross-legged on the table top at the other end and smiling. Even Pendal's mouth opened slightly and then was closed. She stopped resting her hand on the great table and moved slowly to the Head of Table chair and pulled the chair further from table and gestured to the man to sit. He looked fearful and backed away.

"Do not fear, no fear should be here, please sit," she asked gently. Oskar, the officers and

Pendal watched as the man slowly and deliberately overcame his fear and sat cautiously in the chair and rested his back against the spot where the Emperor rested his. "Please…" said Pendal moving to another chair and lifting it out so as not to make a scraping noise and then sat facing the harvester. "Please tell me what happens here?" She asked.

The harvester looked at Pendal, ignoring the others. "The Emperor comes here and sometimes to one of the other two villages close by. He comes when he wants to hide from things in the southern regions. He started coming shortly after the Grey Priest appeared." The harvester paused. "I think he sent her to make the changes that ended the goodness in this village and turned it into a cruel one for the likes of me. She denounced the Village Protector in the square and he was found dead the next day, then the men who operated the ferry boat and the horses on the other side of the river left. They were scared out of their minds. They said they had been visited by a demon. But the ones that kill travelers and steal their wealth have been safe all this time." He spoke slowly and took time to perfectly form his words. "Then we were told we were unsuitable for this place and thrown out." He stopped again and this time looked around at Oskar and the officers. He nodded towards them, "you are not safe," he said, nodding again.

"Tell me, am I safe?" Asked Pendal.

The harvester studied her, looking deeply into her eyes, "yes, you are safe, very safe."

"Thank you," said Pendal for the assurance. "Do you know when the Emperor will come here next?" Asked Pendal.

The harvester frowned and sighed at the question, he looked at the others who had come in with him, "Will they be safe?" He asked Pendal.

"Yes, she said, they will be safe," replied Pendal.

"The Emperor usually comes around this time, perhaps in five or six Day Risings, he will not be here when the white flakes start falling from the sky though." He frowned and sighed again and looked over at the others. Pendal could tell he was getting fidgety, and want to be with the others and rest.

"Two simple questions, can you answer them? Asked Pendal. She received a nod and continued, "Who cleans this place, it is so spotless? They do a very good job of it."

The harvester ran his hand over the table and then he looked around the room at the floors and chairs that he could see, "We do, the harvesters. If we do good work the Grey

Priest lets us use the stone in the square to eat." Then he leaned towards Pendal, "You think it is good work? Well, I thank you! The Grey Priest made us start from the side rooms and the bathing area and kitchen, we work back towards the door and then out. She watched everything." He sat back in his chair. "You said one more question."

"When the Emperor comes here, how many men does he bring?" Asked Pendal.

The harvester stayed motionless, staring at the cot across from where he was sitting. Pendal was about to ask him again when he suddenly replied. "May be ten or twelve, no more than there are cots for." Then the harvester rose from his chair and started to walk over to the others. The oldest was now sitting on the edge of his cot eating slowly from a bowl one of the others had brought for him.

"I am sorry, one more question. Where does the Emperor sleep when he is here?" She asked.

The harvester replied by pointing at the cot he had been staring at. Pendal thanked him and looked up as some of the other harvesters started to nervously enter.

Pendal rose and went around the end of the table, as she passed Oskar, he looked up at her and quietly asked, "Do you believe him?"

Pendal didn't even break her stride and did not look at him, "Yes, of course I do!"

Pendal stood at the entrance to the space where the cot lay pushed up against the far wall. It was the same form and contained the same cot as all the others Pendal noted except the cot was against the far wall, away from the entrance, where the others had the cot close to the entrance. Placing the cot this way gave a little more privacy. It was also the only cot that had four legs. All the other cots were attached to the wall on one long side, which meant they only needed two legs on the other side.

Pendal left the space and called over a lighting globe and turned it to high. The small space was clearly illuminated and she could see where the cot had been fastened to the wall before being removed and given two extra legs. She walked over to the old fastenings in the wall and kicked them lightly with her boot one sounded normal, the other, hollow. Pendal stood back and Oskar waved the officers to work. They moved quickly into the space, pulling out blades so they could cut and open the wall fastening.

Soon they were looking at two narrow trays that had been resting on ledges hacked into the wall. In one were several Imperial seals, one being that of the Emperor personally.

The other tray held a small blade with a sheath that was intricately engraved in gold with the Emperors personal seal. As they studied them, they had not noticed the harvester return to the table.

"Oh, you are looking for hidden things, things in the walls and such. Maybe the floors?" He asked.

Pendal looked up, "Yes, are there more? Can you show us?" She asked.

His face seemed to light up, "Of course I can, I know them all." He started to move around the entire space with Pendal, Oskar and one of the officers following, Oskar had sent the other for additional officers to help. By the time that officer returned with six others, a collection of blades and three projectile weapons, seals from three great and four minor houses, and a store of preserved food had been uncovered.

Oskar studied the seals as the officers removed the weapons; the food Pendal instructed was left for the harvesters.

Oskar placed the seals in a pouch held by one of the officers and instructed him to take several men and ride back to the capital and give them to the High Protector. He was also to describe the circumstances in which they were uncovered. He turned to Pendal, "We knew a few of the great houses were aligned with the Emperor, we did not know of those four minor houses, the High Protector will also be interested in all that has gone on here."

"Don't forget," she looked at Oskar and then the officer, "there are two more villages, they could be the same as here. And we will need to replace the priests in all three villages, word must be sent to my Garfan monastery about this." She said.

Pendal looked over at the harvesters, more had arrived and they were moving in with enthusiasm and ease, it was as if they had never really left. As she and Oskar stepped out in to Day Rise, she inhaled deeply and slowly let out the breath and then repeated. As she repeated for a third breathe she thanked Callar, wherever his soul was, for his guidance to come to Pletke.

Oskar looked at the bright Day Rise light pouring through a gap between two buildings and landing on some plantings across from the entrance, "yes we need more troops and we need to clean out the other two villages." He said pausing to suck air in through his teeth. "You do not need to do that."

Excitement

Oskar sat with his chin resting on his hands curled on top of his stick.

"You do not seem excited?" He asked.

Pendal shrugged, and moved her body armour into a slightly different position. "A Demis Priest!" She looked at Oskar, "that is one level below the High Priest in the Garfan Order. I would be soooo much younger than all the others at that level." She drew out the word "so" to emphasize her words. "It seems they and the Order of 1 are competing to elevate me to higher and higher rank now that they know my bloodline." In front of Pendal on the table lay the proclamation brought just a few time periods ago at great speed by couriers and by three Garfan priests who would replace the Grey Priests in the afflicted villages.

The wind now played with the corners of the document but could not move it, a heavy rock in the centre held it firmly to the table.

"It may not be just your bloodline, it's what you are doing and what you stand for out here, in the real world," said Oskar. He looked around at the village, it was happier and more vibrant, "whatever happened at the monastery over the years made you into a special kind of person and that person is also a priest and an Empress. No one here know you are an Empress." He said looking at Pendal.

Pendal was silent, she needed time to meditate and clear her mind of the worries and concerns that were accumulating. After the judgment at the first village the other two in the region had been cleared of similar "Grey Priests" who were not part of any order, they where there to suppress and manage the local inhabitants so the Emperor and his followers could come and go without much risk of being upset or captured by VodaKhan forces. They did this by fear, a strange concocted religion, and outright murder.

Oskar had left it to Pendal to decide whether to replace the Grey Priests from the Order of Garfan or from the Order of 1. In spite of all she had endured at the monastery, she chose Garfan. She was not sure what a new priest might have to endure and possibly fight for, a Garfan priest would be able to endure and fight if she had to. Pendal had also grown up in the Garfan order and in spite of it all she was more Garfan than any other order.

A cloth worker appeared to Oskar's right carrying Pendal's robes. She bowed deeply and held out the robes for inspection. Oskar had insisted that Pendal's elevated priestly station be recorded on the black collar of her robes immediately. They had found a local worker to make the changes. The collar was now edged with a broad gold thread and the priest symbol had been changed to that of a Demis Priest. The blue and hold rope braiding at her waist was still blue and gold, but a maroon band had been added to the gold. The cuffs had been edged with black and the same thick gold thread; the symbols on her collar were replicated on the black cuffs.

Pendal slipped the robes over her armour and studied the symbols at her cuffs and the change in the braided rope was subtle but meaningful. She thanked Oskar and the cloth worker. Pendal took the rock from the proclamation and was about to fold it up rather than roll it and put it in a hidden pocket of her robes when Oskar reached out and took it from her hands and rolled it up, resealing it as he did. "This is for your history." He said.

She looked at him, "You too!" She exclaimed.

Oskar rocked back in his seat as he prepared to stand and spoke without looking at Pendal, "You said yourself, there are very few Garfan priests out in the world, I would estimate with the three we now have in the villages and yourself, there are four." He paused, "and there is no history of Garfan priests judging others, you are probably the first, and no monastery record of a priest becoming a blade smith for almost one thousand cycles, you also said that yourself." He stood and looked at Pendal, "they are not so much celebrating by your bloodline, you are giving Garfan a whole new perspective of the world and the world a new view of Garfan, people like myself have a new and better regard for the order. Now, let's leave, we have a long way to go and a lot to do."

Thick Trees

Pendal looked down from behind thick trees on the rim of the river valley, the winding river, the plantings on the thick nutritious ground soil and the waving reeds at the sides of the river made it hard to see on occasions where the river ended and the ground soil started. There was an occasional cart traveling along the route beside the river, the same route she had been traveling on when she met the harvester.

Second moon reflected off the river and the glow of lights from the far village competed to brighten the night's blackness.

It would take time for the reinforcements sent by the High Protector to arrive, the forces they had were on battle footing, no camp fires no groupings of more than two or three soldiers, but never the less the dispersed soldiers formed two staggered rings of defense with a smaller fortress core inside of which were Pendal and Oskar. Pendal had protested the arrangement, she was much more comfortable sleeping under a simple sleeping clothe by a log and hidden under some branches from near by trees than in the "core" as the leading officer referred to it.

Pendal turned to sit on a near by log, closed her eyes and started to breathe deeply, exhaling slowly so as to clear her mind of all the toxic things that happened and which diverted her attention from the NOW. As she sat and breathed in and out, her worries went with the exhaled breathe. Her mind became lighter and connected with the animals and growing things that surrounded her. She felt the warmth of the animals breathing as they came out of the bushes and trees to see what was the source of this new energy in their woodland.

Her hands tingled along the edges and then her palms became warm, and then hot. A small ground animal scrambled up the side of the log and along it and on to her lap and then into her hand, it sniffed the air in Pendal's direction. Then it lay down and curled up to go to sleep in her palm.

Silence sat next to Pendal on the log and brought out many more animals, the largest being a Kovanor. Like a large, very powerful dog, the Kovanor is the only natural enemy of a Vanmor and killed them frequently. It walked slowly and silently towards Pendal and sat next to her, it sniffed at the small ground animal in her hand and then it rested its heavy head on her lap and she stroked it head with her eyes closed.

When Pendal opened her eyes the small ground animal was gone and the Kovanor also, Third Moon was high in the night sky. Pendal felt cleansed and relaxed. And, she had lots of memories, her guiding spirits always entered her thoughts when she slept like this and when she cleared her mind like now, they left behind images, thoughts, ideas and things that would help her and she could remember for the future. Her mind was full of rich, wonderful ideas and things to do.

Pendal slipped down the side of the ridge and into the core defense. Some leafy tree branches had been set up to cover the earth and to provide some warmth, Oskar slept a few feet away. Unused to sleeping on the ground he had nearly four times the amount of branches than Pendal had. She was asleep again before she was fully stretched out.

Pendal was up and eating cold food on the log she had sat on just a few time periods before. It was that still time between the setting of the Third Moon and the First Day Rise. The Kovanor was back and she was hand feeding him small amounts of the food the soldiers were eating at their posts. Pendal was offered a small burner to heat the food but when she asked if all would have a burner, she was told no, so she refused it. The small ground animal was also back, sitting on the log beside her, he received small amounts of her food as well.

Oskar surveyed the scene with a mixture of emotions. The Kovanor caused him great alarm, but he also could see that Pendal was not afraid of the animal, indeed she seemed to be treating it like a dog that had been domesticated and the animal was returning her sentiment with almost playful love. The ground animal was less of a concern, but he knew that if it felt threatened one of its defenses was to jump at an attackers face and eyes.

As Pendal finished eating the animals left and Oskar was able to join her on the log.

"I knew you were there, you could have come over at anytime," She said.

Oskar just shook his head in response. He turned is attention to the river now darkened by the lack of light from neither moon nor sun. Away in the far distance, a few lights shimmered in the air from Pletke. "The reinforcements should arrive later today," he said quietly so as not to disturb the atmosphere of quiet all around them. It had been a long time since he had been in "the field" like this and he had forgotten some of the magical moments the day offered that he mostly slept through until now.

"My family have to be safe, the NighT Guardian, Cavahn and the others, they have to be brought north and protected." Her voice was quiet but firm. "I will go south and collect them."

Oskar studied the clouds to the south and the feint golden glow of Day Rise on them. "My answer to that is that we will arrange it, in fact I have already started making arrangements, we must be careful. At the opening of the senate your maternal bloodline was clear, your paternal bloodline however remained a secret. That secrecy is the biggest advantage we have." He continued to look at the fiery colours spreading across the sky. "We will bring them here one by one, through separate teams and following separate routes, they can only meet up when they are returned to you."

Oskar made circles with his stick in the dirt, "The hardest part of this will be your sisters in the Black Legion." As he stopped speaking, Oskar tapped the ground soil, sending small pieces of it in different directions.

Pendal sensed the tension on Oskar about what she was asking. "Would it make it easier if we created a situation where I could kill the Emperor?" She asked.

Oskar had considered the option more than once. Creating a situation where it would be possible seemed so difficult as to be impossible. Such an act would need immediate military intervention to ensure those who were tied to the Emperor and those who hoped and schemed to obtain some advantage by the change of ruler could be controlled. There was also the problem of VodaKhan gold. Oskar knew in his heart and mind that Pendal would not need such shipments when she came to rule but there were many along the journey of a shipment who had become wealthy and powerful. They to were a threat both to Pendal and to VodaKhan.

A storm was coming

The wind had started to pick up and the clouds had grown thicker and darker, the surface of the river was no longer calm, it was covered in ripples and at the edges where the liquid touched the ground soil it was frothy from trying to climb out.

Pendal looked at the fiery cloud colours and the light of Pletke, a growing storm had covered the Day Rise start behind a thick covering but the clouds were still fiery and the lights of Pletke were still bright. Suddenly she stood up, as she understood what she was seeing. "Oskar, Pletke is burning!" She exclaimed loudly and forcefully.

Oskar was caught off guard and looked up at Pendal and then at the storm clouds and then at Pletke far off in the distance. He struggled to get to his feet, as he did Pendal heading for the camp passed him. "What are you doing? You cannot go to Pletke! We do not have enough men!" He shouted after her, he moved as quickly as he could to follow her but she was already in the core by the time he came over the ridge. He started waving his stick and shouting to attract the attention of his men, they must not go and Pendal must not go. No one must go.

As he slipped and slithered down the slope he managed to keep his feet and shout instructions at the same time. As he walked and hobbled in to the core a soldier handed him the reigns to his horse. It was ready to take him to Pletke.

On the route to Pletke, Oskar finally caught up with Pendal.

She was not that far ahead when it was all said and done and she had sent not one but two riders via different routes for reinforcements, the reinforcements mounted on horseback would have to ride hard to catch up but they would. Those on foot would be far behind.

Sensibly, but still risky the leading officer had split their force, some were with Pendal and Oskar on the route next to the river, the others were following a track, it could not be called a route, through the late field crops. Because it would take them longer to arrive at Pletke those riding on the route were proceeding more slowly than if they had been riding hard to get to Pletke quickly. There was a sense of the inevitable; the fires had been started sometime before Day Rise start so had burned through much of the village centre by the time everyone had left camp. A village the size of Pletke should be able to quench one, two or three fires in houses or buildings, the fact the town seemed to be burning meant either the fires had been set and spread or no one was there to stop them.

Liquid water had started to fall from the sky and it pinged and danced on the surface of the river making the surface dance and splash, it also made the surface of the route slippery.

It was cool to the skin and refreshing. It drenched everyone's hair.

As they rode, the smell of burning came on the wind in small puffs at first but as they got closer, it became more persistent and stronger.

The route matched the twists and turns of the river, as it finally turned toward Pletke they faced into the wind passing over the village and the smell of burning and destruction became overwhelming. For a time Pendal let the horse follow the route allowing her to concentrate inwardly on her guiding spirits, preparing herself for what tests and pain would soon be assaulting her senses. This would be like nothing she had ever seen or felt before.

The liquid from the sky grew thicker and the drops bigger and heavier. The temperature in the air around them dropped suddenly making it cold and bitter.

Ahead a man, limping and waving his arms, came towards them from Pletke, as he got closer Pendal recognized him as the harvester she had befriended when she met him carrying a sack of river creatures over his shoulder.

Pendal dismounted and just caught the harvester as he tripped on a small rut in the route; he was covered in dark black fire ash, which mixed with blood from a gash on his leg that caused him to limp. He smelled of fire and burning and death.

Pendal sat him on a rock and gave him a flask of river liquid, which he drank from thirstily, his lungs filled and expelled air in huge quantities as Pendal tried to settle him down so he could answer questions. She started washing and bandaging his wounded leg. From the shape and angle of the wound she could see it was done with a long blade, she had been cut with a long blade once, on her right leg. The technique was to injure one or both of the opponent's legs with a long blade so they could not move, or move only with difficulty, then question them. By the time the questioning was over, they would either have bled out and died, or need to be killed with a short blade.

The harvester was finally coming back into the present, he was no longer being threatened, wounded and cut, buildings around him were not burning and people were not dying. He looked fascinated at Pendal tending him and the cleaning and dressing of his wound. "Thank you… thank you, I knew you would return, we need you desperately." He said half crying, and his chest heaving as he looked back along the route in the direction of Pletke.

At the Edge of Pletke

At the edge of Pletke, Pendal dismounted.

The home where she dismounted was still intact but there were no people; in the fenced areas at the back of the house animals rooted for food in and on the ground but otherwise went about their business as if nothing had happened. One of them saw her and approached looking for fresh food to be put out. It made loud noises, noises associated with people and being fed by them. There was a large cask of food by the side of the fence, Pendal picked it up several handfuls and spread the feed along the edge of the fencing so the animal could get to it. Soon the others sensed the food and came over to share in the bounty. As Pendal moved around the fenced area, the animals were busy feeding and no longer making noise.

She scouted from house to house, the closer to the village centre the worse the conditions of the buildings and she started to see animals killed for no other reason than it appeared they could be.

And then, dead people. All killed with a long blade, often in the back and left to bleed to death. The heavy sky liquid was washing away the blood from the bodies.

Then the fluttering of a gold and purple rag, a piece of a tunic, or a cloak worn around the upper body; Pendal pulled it from the stiffening hand that held it and opened it fully.

Oskar, huffing and puffing came up behind her, she held it out for him to look at. He flipped the material over so he could see both sides; he held out the side that showed part of a house crest, "this is part of the crest of one of the minor houses, the same as one of the houses we identified in that building the harvesters moved back in to." He stopped to look at the material in closely. "The work on this material is very good, and it is expensive work, this was torn from a member of the house, not a soldier." He said and wrapped it up and put it in his pocket.

Suddenly a door in the house in front of them burst open, smashing against the wall as it did so, out stepped a tall thin man wearing a gold and purple robe, a corner missing from his right sleeve. He was dragging a young boy by the hair, the boy was bleeding heavily from his mouth and one eye was beaten closed, blood came from a gash on his cheek. The boy's hands and feet tried desperately to help him stand but the tall thin man pulled the boy this way and that, preventing the him from being steady long enough to be able to recover his balance. Finally the boy was thrown to the ground, the tall thin man cursed the boy loudly and repeatedly and waved the torn sleeve and then he kicked the boy hard in the ribs, breaking several.

Then there was silence.

Except for the groans of the young boy on the ground there was silence.

The boy twisted to look up at his tormentor with his one good eye. The tall thin man hovered over him with a large handful of the boys blood soaked hair in one hand was no longer standing, he was on his knees, much closer to the boy, a blade was buried to the handle in one side of the man's neck with its black blade jutting out sharply from the other side. His features were fixed on some distant scene and did not move or change. A slender feminine hand appeared in the boy's vision and grasped the blade handle and jerked it from the man's neck. Then a second slender hand appeared and took hold of the man's hair as tightly as the boy's had been held and jerked the head back. The first hand drew the blade across the man's throat to reveal the spine. A heavy boot placed in the man's chest pushed the body away from the boy.

Strong hands from one of the soldiers helped the boy sit up against a fence post as Pendal went inside. The house was smashed, everything was broken, furniture, eating and cooking bowls, a cask of fresh liquid had been over turned. Decorations on the wall had been torn down and broken, there were bloodstains in one corner where the boy had been caught and beaten. There was no one else in the house.

Oskar was handing a flask of liquid to the soldier helping the boy as she came out. Oskar gestured at the body on the ground, "He is head of one of the four minor houses." He said.

The soldier stood up and addressed Pendal and Oskar. "The boy says there were four riders, all in fine garb. He had seen them before when the Emperor comes here. When they found the changes we made they went on a rampage, killing everyone they saw and burning buildings around the village square, some of the building burned with people inside."

Pendal looked at the piece of fabric Oskar had taken out and was holding and handed it to the soldier, "Looks like we have to collect more fabric!" She said.

"There is more," said the soldier. "The four riders had with them several others but he knows nothing of them."

A wind picked up as Pendal and the others entered the village centre, it was clearing out the smoke and the liquid falling from the sky was persistent and heavy and had started to quench the fires. The smell of burning was now mixed with the damp wet smell of burned wood, possessions, and blood draining from dead bodies.

The soldier identified horse prints in the ground soil, which were now filling with sky liquid. Long blades had cut down the villages from riders on horseback. Short blades had cut some down in or at the entrance to their homes and a few at the back as they tried to escape. The unarmed villagers had been pursued with relentless death and destruction.

As they continued their search Pendal and the soldiers were quiet and stealthy. Although they saw no one, there were sounds, sound of someone moving ahead of them searching for things to remove. Tantalizing shapes, perhaps a horse or a person, disappearing around a corner but not there when they reached it.

Her senses were tuned to a high level, her hearing, her eyesight, her ability to smell and separate the smell of an enemy from amongst all the horrors around her.

The sound of a pet animal being butchered sent Pendal through an open window, as she looked up and sensed the plodding of a heavy person she hid under the stairs behind its broken hand rail laying on the floor. Through a crack in the steps she could see the elaborate robes of a Minor house float down the stairs, they were stained with sky liquid, mud, and blood, the wearer was already judged and condemned.

The appearance of a VodaKhan soldier at the door to the house was all Pendal needed, the House member froze dropping the pet animals head as he reached for his long blade. Using the edge of a step as a hand hold Pendal came out from hiding under the stairs and sprang into the air driving her blade through the mans head.

The House member was dead before the soldier had full control of his long blade. As Pendal strode past him, she gave him a torn off cuff to put with the others.

At the end of the search they found a few of the murdering riders celebrating at one of the wealthier homes. Pendal led a group of soldiers in a quick, effective, and ruthless dispatching of those who had abused and killed the villagers.

Carnage

The village square was carnage.

Human carnage.

It was despair.

The village square was covered in bodies of young and old, men and women. The Garfan priest who had only been assigned to the village a short while ago was dead and her body hung from the front of the place Pendal and Oskar had spent time eating at before they left the village in her care.

She had fought bravely to deal with the threat to the village and the villagers; there were several dead from blade wounds in front of her body. As with Callar at the route stop, the dead were not soldiers, they were robbers and thieves.

A senior officer said the number of horses found that did not belong to the village matched the number of dead criminals they were seeing. Horses belonging to members of the minor Imperial houses were decorated with the colours of their house; the colours the horses wore matched the pieces of highly decorated material taken from garments worn by "riders in fine garb," as the boy had called them.

"Are you sure there is not a horse we have not accounted for, one perhaps suitable for an Emperor?" Asked Oskar as he looked at Pendal, they were both hoping there would be a horse that was somehow identifiable as belonging to the Emperor and indicating he was here but had not been found.

To that Pendal simply said, "If he were hiding in VodaKhan, his horse might not be anything special, it is only when you want to be seen as the Emperor, do you worry about the quality of the horse you sit on." Oskar nodded in frustration.

Pendal took a stool and placed it behind the post from which the young priest hung and cut her down. Her body was propped against the post with her head slightly forward and her hands folded in her lap. She looked as if she were taking a rest. Pendal, Oskar and the officer stood looking at her. "Long blades, she was killed with three thrusts of one or more long blade, she could not defend against them with her blade." He said.

Oskar looked sternly at Pendal, "You must have a long blade you must!" He said earnestly. "Have you trained with one?" He asked.

Pendal looked at the body and then at the number of bodies in the square. "Yes, it was mandatory. I used to be as good with a long blade as you have seen with me with these blades." She said turning to look at Oskar and the officer and patting the sheath at her waist.

At the far end of the village square the officer leading the soldiers who had followed the track through the fields appeared with twenty or so soldiers. They moved through the carnage towards Oskar and Pendal, slowly, being careful not to disturb the villager's bodies. Oskar looked at him cautiously he was worried that so much of their forces were now in or very close to the village, if there were to be another attack…

"What of the reinforcements, how many did the High Protector send?" He demanded.

"We have a full Legion, Ten Cohorts. Two overlapping rings are being set up around and the village, each ring is a cohort, a cohort has been sent to the each of the other two villages." He said in a flat factual tone. "The remaining cohorts are dispersed to the north of us." He hesitated for a moment, "we found quite a few villagers in the fields, they had tried to escape into the plantings but were ridden down by men on horseback and killed with long blades."

Oskar nodded, "A legion, that is a lot of men and a great force to support us, good." He said.

"There is more," said the officer, "we caught two riders with long blades trying to escape." Oskar looked at him sharply.

The officer nodded "We disarmed them and captured them." He said.

Oskar looked that the bloodied square as the Sky liquid continued to poor down. "Make sure those animals do not escape, we have many questions for them." He said in an increasingly bitter tone.

"Sir!" Said the officer. "When the men caught the riders and seeing what happened in the fields, they broke the captives legs. They will not be escaping." He turned on his heal and started to walk toward his men.

The two riders they caught were a thief and robber and a high-ranking member of one of the four houses they had identified earlier. Now both were questioned relentless and strong herbs applied, as with Callar, to bring out the information they needed.

The emperor was not with them.

He had schemed with the Grand Leaders of the four minor houses that came north with him regularly to gather a band of robbers and thieves used to violent work and deeds. Their plan was to use Pletke as base, first to rob and steal from the village and then the other two close by villages.

A few gold shipments from VodaKhan to the Emperor came overland and not by sea, Pletke was an ideal place to rob these shipments and the Emperor had provided details of two shipments that were to pass near Pletke before the winter set in. The shipments were to be robbed and the gold brought south where the Emperor would split the value with the four minor houses and deny the gold had been brought to him, VodaKhan would have to replace the missing valuable metal.

When the murderous group had arrived and seen the changes to the village and the resistance of the Garfan priest the intent to rob the village became an orgy of killing and burning. All had taken part in it, the tall thin man Pendal had dispatched enjoyed it the most.

A Dinning Table

Oskar looked down the long dinning table in the harvester's building, the remains of the men's first meal of Day Rise still rested in bowls at their seating positions. The building was untouched by burning and carnage because the members of the four houses had planned to continue it use it as their private living space, their bags had been found at the door and thoroughly searched. "The High Protector is sending four more legions, two will strengthen the border and one will be with us. The last legion will be held back in reserve so it can move to any position to provide support." He sipped at some river liquid and then turned to face Pendal.

Pendal sat back in her chair, her eyes fixed on two long blades and a mid blade set out on the table in front of her. All three blades were of the finest black metal like her own but would have to be weighted and balanced for her, the handles would have to be changed to better suit her slender but incredibly strong hands. Having the armorer of an entire legion at her disposal, she had shown him how the NighT Guardian had modified her blade sheathes to sharpen them as she removed and replaced them. He could not replicate the fine stone that did this work, it did not exist in the north, but he could replicate the action with something else.

Pendal had determined she would carry one long blade, and a mid blade, something between a long blade and the hand blades she preferred. The sheath arrangement for the additional blades must not hinder her access to the blades at her front and at her back. But she could not help but reflect that sitting there as she was, with throwing blades in her boots, a blade in front and at her back, wearing incredibly refined body armour, she was hardly a priest anymore. She voiced her thoughts to Oskar.

"You are a warrior priest, there have been such in the past, here in VodaKhan. It was said they carried spirit guides in one hand, righteousness and purpose in the other and love and learning in their voice." He looked at Pendal but realized she had not heard the words; she was somewhere else in her thoughts.

There was a tapping at the door, the guards outside wanted to know if they should let the old harvesters back in. Oskar saw no reason to keep them outside and agreed.

The old harvesters filed into the room and sat at their places. The old one she had met at the fountain and promised to observe his passing led them; he sat quietly beside Pendal. He said nothing; he looked at the long blades, the mid blade and Pendal's face. "Pendal," he said in a quiet voice, "you are in my seat."

Pendal looked at him over her shoulder, "I am sorry, I will move." Her tone was dry, tired and without the essence of energy she usually spoke with.

"No," said the old man. "You should stay in my seat, for a while anyway. I asked you to observe my passing and you agreed. Those words made me feel loved and cared for. When these men arrived and started burning and killing I hoped you would come to be with me at my last moments." He paused to look Pendal in the eyes, "But instead you came with good soldiers and did away with these evil people. I am here now to tell you that you are in my seat instead of being face down in the mud, and with the blood of many others." He stopped talking, and reached out and took Pendal's hand and started rubbing it like a parent would rub a child's hand. Then he looked around at the others sitting at the table, all were looking at Pendal, "You came and blessed the village with words not long ago, and today you blessed us all with life, and many others who escaped into the fields." As he stood, he looked at the others, "we must remake our meal," as he said that the others slowly got to their feet and collected their bowls and shuffled to the kitchen.

He looked down at Pendal, "You are welcome to eat with us, but please sit over there," he pointed to two vacant seats, "and take your long blades with you." Then he gathered his bowls and shuffled to the kitchen.

Pendal gathered up her blades and she and Oskar did as they were told.

The Forge

"Well?" Asked Oskar as he watched Pendal walk away from the forge.

The Forge Master stood next to him wiping his hands with a clean rag, he was removing the smoke ash and sweat from them before he answered Oskar. "I have never been in the presence of someone so intense." The Forge Master turned to watch Pendal, "she knows every little thing about those blades. Every hair's width of the blade the cutting edge, the hand guard, the handle, and the hand butt. The balance she had me put in them is finer than any I have ever produced." He turned to look at Oskar, "and I have created the finest high competition blades." He turned back into his forge shaking his head, and sat down on a stool exhausted.

Oskar followed him into the forge and felt the heat from the roaring main forge and the secondary forges, each operating at different temperatures. On the floor several blade handles lay thrown around and amongst them blade weights, handle bindings and animal skin for sheathes. By a secondary forge strips of special steel used to sharpen even harder steel lay cut in different odd lengths. He sat on a stool close by the Forge Master and used his stick to flip the metal handles and weights, with the tip of his stick he picked up some animal skin remains used for the sheathes and examined it.

The Forge Master found a clean corner of the cloth and started to wipe his forehead and his face. "You say she is a priest?" He asked Oskar.

"A Demis Priest, of the Garfan order." Oskar replied.

The Forge Master looked at Oskar, "Really, a Demis Priest, that is a level below the High priest, and the Garfan order you say!" he shuddered as he said the name. "Now I understand the intensity in her." He paused for a moment and threw the cloth into the forge and it caught fire immediately. "I had a friend who went to that order when he was very young. His parents thought that giving up a son to the order was a good deed. I met the son a few cycles later, Garfan say they do not produce blade smiths or warrior priests but in him and Pendal they produce warriors who are called priests."

Oskar slowly stood and took one look around the forge and then addressed the Forge Master. "So, there is nothing else you can do with those blades?" He asked.

The Forge Master looked around the forges and the remnants of handles and weights on the floor. "I offered to engrave and decorate the blades but she refused. She said the blades were working blades and decoration did not suit her." He looked up at Oskar. "Those other blades she carries, she showed them to me, they are equally perfect, and they too are undecorated. All the blades she now carries are perfect." The Forge Master rocked on his stool as Oskar patted him on the shoulder as he walked out.

Calming

The camp busied itself with the military duties it was used to carrying out and a mix of other responsibilities connected with people from the village. Many more than Pendal realized had survived the attack by running into the fields and hiding in the late plantings. It was those that trusted in hiding in their homes and trusting in the men from the four minor houses that had died or come close to dying as the boy they had first rescued.

Pendal's tent was at the centre of the camp, she sat and rested, pulling in all the calming influences she could gather from her spirits and the late season song birds in the trees and bushes by the camp. Guards were placed at arms length around it, Oskar and the officers were not taking for granted that those who meant anyone, especially her ill, had been caught or killed. The two they had captured were on their way under heavy guard to he capital where more questioning awaited them. One guard carried pieces of cloth torn from the sleeves of the four minor houses that had started the massacre.

The sky liquid had stopped falling several time periods ago and Pendal wore new immaculately prepared robes, as she sat she turned her attention to the sacred symbols on her cuffs, saying the prayer that went with each helped to cleanse her energy centers and her mind. As she did her mind closed to the noise and business of the camp and floated in a clean bright white space. In front of her letters and pictures came in and out of focus as if they floated on a milky white liquid, she could reach out and stir them, she could push them under the surface of the milky liquid and they would bob up somewhere else in her vision. As she stirred and played with the letters, some started to stick together, as she stirred some more, the letters attracted more letters and still more. She pushed the block of letters under the surface and they reappeared still together but with more letters attached. Then she looked and there were no more free letters, the letters not attached together were sinking and were gone. She was left with letters that formed a sacred word; she looked at the word, it was familiar, she had studied it many times at the monastery. The word meant many things, to be prepared or to have prepared, but it could also be a drive to action, to start something for which preparation was needed or had been completed.

As she looked at the word it started to rotate, slowly at first and then more violently, then it slowed and something, a symbol, appeared in the middle of the letters, she could not miss it, it was red, bright red. The symbol was used to organize writing; it could only be used with certain words like the one she had been looking at. It both split the meaning of the word into two but joined them and added its own. It split the meaning of the word into preparation which was to the left of the symbol and meant what was required to be prepared had been done, completed, and a call to action that which was on the right of the symbol. The red colour of the symbol meant the call to action must begin, it was an imperative.

As she stared at the bright redness of the imperative she became aware of a disturbance to the right. She smiled; a small figure was swimming back and forth, back and forth. Then a second figure appeared. The first swimmer bumped into the word and stopped swimming and looked up at the letter it had bumped into and climbed up on to it and seemed happy at what it could see. The other swimmer bumped into the word repeatedly but continued trying to swim. For a moment the swimmer rolled over on his back, a mouth in a round face opened as if gasping for air, and then the swimmer rolled back over and continued swimming.

The figure standing on the word became aware of Pendal looking down and turned to look up and playfully waved at her and then pointed at the word. Pendal stopped breathing for a moment, the small figure standing on the word for action and waving at her was her father, the NighT Guardian!

Smoke from a nearby campfire drifted over Pendal's face and the smell made her sneeze and cough.

This shattered the word and what she saw in her mind's eye and brought her back to the world of noise and smells, good and bad. To her surprise, Moon Rise had begun; already the white light of first moon was covering the camp with its pale pure glow.

When she had sat down outside her tent there had been nothing in front of her.

While she meditated, a table had been added and food set out with fresh river liquid waited for her to return to the present, the physical world where she sat. She breathed deeply and could now smell the food in front of her. One by one she opened the bowl lids and took in the nutritious smells. Finally, she took the lids off the small bowls of spices.

Slowly, one by one, she started mixing the spices and the food. She looked up. Oskar and several senior officers had started to gather, they brought with them map rolls, pads for writing and writing instruments. They brought with them devices to calculate.

As they sat they nodded to Pendal, the deference was real and genuine. Though watching her eat hungrily of such fiercely spiced food raised the eye browse of those not used to seeing, or smelling it.

"It is time," said Oskar, "to bring your family out from the southern regions." He watched as the officers started unfurling their maps and placing weights on them to keep them flat. Lighting globes had been brought over to illuminate the table.

"What has changed?" Asked Pendal.

Addressing the officers Oskar started to speak, "We have a critical mass of the right kind and type of soldiers…"

"What has changed?" Asked Pendal, interrupting Oskar and sitting back in her chair, as she did so she brought a bowl of food close to her chest and started rapidly spooning its contents into her mouth.

Oskar turned to look at Pendal with a slightly annoyed expression on his face. Between the two of them they were used to speaking quickly and with a certain brutal frankness, that left nothing to the imagination, and with it etiquette and debate were casualties lying bleeding beside their interaction.

"Our spies tell us the prison where Sovan the Dekar Emperor was held is now empty, it serves the Emperor no purpose. Your sister K'ola has been returned to field operations with the Imperial Black Legion, but she is sick and being cared for by your healer sister Vella."

Pendal looked at Oskar and the officers over the edge of her bowl as she considered the information. "The prison was also where The Emperor stored his gold and held court. I find it hard to imagine it serves him no purpose anymore," said Pendal as she picked a piece of food from between her teeth. "Are your spies VodaKhan born or paid spies from the south?" She asked.

"VodaKhan born and raised", replied Oskar. "Are you thinking this might be a trap?" Oskar looked at her over the handle of his stick on which he rested both hands.

"Of course," said Pendal finishing her food and picking up the glass of clear river liquid and sipping from it. "Where are the "field operations K'ola is assigned to and where is Vella?" Pendal asked.

"Slightly to the south of the prison where the NighT Guardian stands guard, it used to be the winter camp of the Seventeenth legion but that legion has been moved to the far south to deal with a rebellion," responded one of the of the officers and indicting on the map the location of the winter camp and the rebellion.

"You are not convinced?" Asked Oskar.

Pendal put down her glass, stood and leaned over the map; she was checking the places the officer indicated. "I walked through large areas of that part of the south, there was no sentiment for rebellion, but like many areas ruled by the Emperor there was unhappiness. Something has changed to make unhappy people become rebellious." She said as she sat down.

Silence joined them at the table; there were no spare seats so it stood looking over them.

Oskar looked as if he were about to speak but stopped. He too seemed unaware of anything that might have changed in the south. It seemed his agents had concentrated on answering the questions he had asked but had not provided him with information about anything else, things that might be of interest. "What are you suggesting?"

Pendal locked eyes with Oskar, "Vella and K'ola are still in the inner castle, I don't think they are prisoners in the way Sovan was, but they have not moved from their location. The Seventeenth was not well trained in putting down rebellions, it was a supply legion, large body of soldiers for general purposes and was equipped with older weaponry if I recall my father speaking of them. To put down a rebellion might be beyond them." She said.

"I have studied drawings of the inner castle and it would be extremely difficult to get through the defenses. If not impossible." Said one of the officers further down the table as she shuffled the maps and diagrams to bring those of the inner castle to the top.

"If you assume you will assault the defenses, I agree," said Pendal, "but we are talking about two people, who if they have a suitable message given to them have the freedom to leave by themselves." Pendal stood and reached over for the map of the prison. "This steep winding road up to the first outer gate would stall an assault, it has been designed to do that. The gate here, at the top is strong but no stronger than at the monastery, it looks more than it is. The inner gate is much further from the outer gate than this map shows, there is almost enough space for a small village here" she paused and pointed at the distance between the inner and outer walls. "The inner gate is far stronger and better defended. The swing bridge inside it over the raging water is almost impossible to assault." She looked at the officers; they were enraptured by the details and observations but clearly needed more.

"The swing bridge is controlled by those on the far side, it is narrow and if you cannot make your way across by the time the bridge goes back into its safe position, you are dead. The bridge, not the defenders will crush you. The river over which its swings over has been made to be violent and dangerous by narrowing it and adding rocks, boulders and other deadly objects."

Pendal paused and sipped from her glass. "I walked the length of the inner defensive wall when I was inside. To North, here," she pointed on the map, "the river is much calmer but it is a sheer cliff up to the top of the inner wall."

Wind tugged at the map and Pendal stopped for a moment as the officers weighted the map before continuing. "In the south, that is the weak point. Men, food and supplies have to get in and out of the inner prison, they do it here, and she pointed at a section at the extreme southern end of the inner defensive wall. "The river is calmer here but most important they have two drop bridges they can lower between the inner and outer defenses, one bridge from the outer wall to the inner, and one from the inner wall to the outer create two separate but effective links. Each is wide enough for broad heavy carts carrying supplies of all kinds as well as people." Pendal paused as the cook brought a plate of sweet roots for them to eat as they talked. Pendal took two of her favourite.

"The other thing about the drop bridges," she looked at the officers, "the defensive walls on both sides is too narrow for any more than a few defenders to engage someone trying to cross from above, the main defenders of these bridges must operate at bridge level." Pendal stuffed the second sweet root into her mouth and reached for a third and sat down. As she slowly ate the third sweet root she watched the officers as they fell into deep concentration.

Oskar leaned across the table, "you don't plan to assault those drop bridges do you?" He asked.

"Of course not!" She exclaimed. Her raised voice got the attention of the officers, "all we need is one maybe two people, agents, specialists in the art of deception and guile." She said as she slowly chewed the first half of the sweet root. "Or maybe we just need one who can follow instructions provided by a Demis Priest," Pendal looked back at Oskar and winked.

A Stone Marker at her Back

Pendal stood with a stone marker at her back.

Moonrise had just begun; First Moon hung low in the sky, giving off its pale clean glow. The air was very cool; winter was not far away, Pendal looked forward to the cold, the snow, but not so much the ice. A vision of rows of herbs she had tended at the monastery came in to her mind.

The stone marker was hewn from the rock in the mountains to the North of VodaKhan; it was thick with blue veins like those in a human body. It marked the boundary between VodaKhan and what they called the "Southern Regions" it seemed to stand with a mixture of disdain, indifference, and mostly a lack of desire to know anything about the south.

As she stood, Pendal was in the Southern Regions. She was well aware there were more than fifty pairs of eyes watching her, and knowing Oskar there would be eyes watching those. Watchers for the watchers he called it.

The decision had been made with some dramatic beating of chests and resistance, but she was here and she was alone at last.

While the eyes would be watching her every move, she would not be leading a VodaKhan army into the south, which was one plan hatched that night not so long ago when she described the defenses and vulnerabilities of the prison.

The idea of making contact with the young round faced Guardian was discussed and dismissed, he was untrained and too eager to gain promotion. He was also unpracticed and there would always be doubts about his ability to carry out the tasks asked of him. Simple questions by a guard at the drop bridges might uncover him and the plan.

They were left with the belief in the report that even if the prison were not closed, the important people, K'ola and Vella had been relocated from there. Cavahn would be at the house by the river along with the NighT Guardian.

Vella had changed his medical records so he could not rejoin the Black Legion. Pendal hated the idea that meant he had been retired from service to the Emperor, she did not know him well enough yet to know how not having duty and ordered tasks to complete would affect him.

Pendal rubbed the neck of her horse. The same horse she had since leading a small party of officers to the route stop where they had captured Callar, its soul was clean and clear, Pendal joined with it whenever they met.

Pendal mounted the horse and they started south.

This journey to her father's home would be different this time; many things would not be as they were before. She was riding a horse, not walking. She was no longer a lowly supplicant; her robes carried the sacred symbols of a Demis Priest and much more. She wore the finest body armour under those robes. The long blade made to her exacting needs was carried in a sheath at her back, the handle was just behind her head; she could draw it with either hand by reaching back over her shoulder rather than carrying it at her waist, the mid blade created for her was also drawn over her shoulder but to her left side and she could use both blades mercilessly.

Pendal had new pride, and a lot of gratitude for her past.

The years at the monastery had been exacting, demanding, and brutal, but she could now see them as being filled with pure white light. There were moments of happiness and sadness, but the training she had excelled in now separated her from those who professed similar skills, they wrapped around her and protected her just as much as the body armour she wore.

As Pendal came over a ridge she looked down and could see a young River Ohm pounding and thrashing with restless energy at the rocks over which it was passing. To her right, several days ride away Moon Rise glinted off the liquid falls the river had passed over from the high mountains. She swung her horse in the direction of the river but not on the main route next to it, she chose a smaller less used route, and she felt her horse agree with the choice.

Pendal rode on through First and Second Moon Rise, only stopping to rest and eat as

Third Moon hit its height in the night sky. She fed and provided liquid for her horse and continued for a few more time periods and then stopped in a thick clump of trees away from the route, the trees would allow her to see what was happening without being seen; even her horse was hidden from view.

Just as when she first walked to the NighT Guardian's home, she used no fire or anything that would give away her resting place. She could only imagine how the soldiers following her and those following them would react.

As she stood beside her horse, rubbing its back and feeding him the grains he liked, all she could think of were nights such as this, just before winter. She had been very young, maybe six cycles as the monastery countered her age, when she first slept out with the pre-winter plantings to protect them from predators. The priest gave her cold food to eat that night; she slept on cold ground, and drank cold liquid for that and many more Moon Risings.

She had made one mistake that first time.

As she slept moisture had drained out of the air and soaked her hair and the ground soil, then there had been a freezing. The moisture on her hair and the ground soil had turned to ice and the ice had locked her head to the ground. A predator had appeared and started to eat the plantings and Pendal had been unable to move to protect them until she ripped the hair from the side of her head and chased it off.

A priest found her crying and head bloodied from the experience and when she recounted what had happened the priest had administered several hard slaps across her face, breaking her lip which bled along with her head.

But the priest had also cared for her bloodied head and lip, dried her tears, and shown her how to avoid such things in the future. She had taught Pendal how to fake the icing of her hair to the ground soil so that she could lure a predator in and kill it before it ate any plantings.

Pendal used that knowledge now as she fell asleep on the uncovered ground soil.

Journey.

Journey, is time.

It takes a traveler time to cover a distance, nor matter how long or short it is, but eventually Pendal was on the wooded trail by the river she and Vella had walked, run, and trained on and where with pain sticks they had killed a vicious wild animal. She recalled the ledge from which it had leapt, and dismounted. She looked over the edge as she walked and eventually could make out the white skull and several bones as well as its skin far below, jammed between some rocks.

Home was not far now.

Behind her she could tell from the sounds of the night animals the soldiers were getting closer, watching and waiting as she moved onward. She had to be cautious, clouds covered most of the sky and the moons were not lighting her way, there was enough in her memory and some feint Moon Rise light coming through gaps in the clouds to allow her to walk with almost magical certainty.

Pendal stopped.

From out of the darkness, suddenly, violently.

Vella.

On the tail.

Breathing heavily, her eyes fierce, face and hair covered in sweat.

She was several steps away but well within the range of Pendal's weapons, especially the long blade she carried on her back. Pendal moved back but gave no sign she was threatened. The soldiers watching had projectile weapons and could easily kill Vella if she threatened Pendal, it was important that they have no cause to use them.

Vella stopped in her stride, her chest heaving from exertion, she reached out for the cliff wall at her side to steady her as her lungs moved her chest ferociously to get air in them. Vella coughed and spat out something that went over the edge of the trail onto the rocks below. She started to cry, loudly and violently. She fell to her knees and hugged herself. Tremendous grief poured from Vella onto the trail, Pendal could not see the tears but she could sense the emotional pain and anguish oozing from Vella's body as clearly as she could see Vella herself. The clouds were clearing and Second Moon's bright clear light shone down from above.

Pendal waited. Vella had to free herself of the pain and sorrow that surrounded her and attached to her. Vella fell silent as her tightly balled fists pounded an erratic rhythm on her thighs.

Pendal moved forward slowly, she braced her mind, her emotions as she reached out to touch Vella. As her hand touched Vella's shoulder something like Sky Light in a storm passed through her body. The violent energy of Vella's grief passed through Pendal and was gone, Pendal did not allow it to remain or take hold of her.

When Pendal held a hand or touched a person at their passing the souls energy, passed over and through her and joined the energy in all life that surrounds the living, Vella's raw pain flowed over and away from Pendal and joined that immense pool of energy.

Vella stopped pounding her fists and her lungs stopped heaving her chest. She slumped, tired and relieved against the cliff wall. Pendal pushed Vella's head back and took a cloth from her pocket and started cleaning her sister's face, as she did, her horse came closer and Pendal took a flask of fresh clear river liquid from its saddle and gave it to Vella to drink. Vella drank slowly and then violently, spilling liquid down her face and on to her chest.

Pendal took Vella under the closest arm, and gave orders, "You will stand, you will do it now and you will walk with me," said Pendal sternly. "You will tell me why you grieve."

Like a broken toy soldier Vella allowed Pendal to lift her to a standing position and turn her around to face down the trail from where she had come. For a while as they walked slowly down the trail Vella did not answer Pendal's orders. Finally Vella spoke, "K'ola is dead." She said with a painful mixture of relief and regret. She coughed up something again and spat it over the trail edge. "That turd of an Emperor killed her." As she said the words, her chest heaved as if she were going to burst out with grief again.

Pendal waited as Vella settled herself she needed information from Vella and she needed Vella to speak clearly so she could understand. "How did he kill her?" She asked quietly.

Vella took several deep breaths and managed to rid herself of her last uncontrolled grief, and could walk now unaided by Pendal. "When Sovan was executed, the Emperor emptied the prison of everyone who was there. He said there was no longer a reason for us to be there. K'ola could not walk without a stick, you saw that, well, her walking became worse after you left. Without any care, he sent her back to field operations." Vella paused, and then continued, "He announced she would lead the rebuilding of the Black Legion." Vella stopped for a moment to look up at Second Moon Rise that was now at its height. "She was killed along with several officers in an accident overseeing junior soldiers from the Seventeenth who had been drafted to the Black Legion." Vella squared her shoulders and started to stride forward but the effort and coordination only lasted for a pew paces and then she was walking again. "She should never have been on the training field that day, but she wanted to see the lack of quality in the draftees…." Vella covered her face with her hands, as she did she rubbed dirt from the ground back on to her face, and rubbed it on her cheeks, "Her body…. All of them…. were cold and stiff when I arrived."

Vella moved to the edge of the trail and fell to her knees, her hands reached out and gripped the rocky edge as she vomited heavily over the side.

Pendal waited.

Finally, Vella placed her right hand on her right knee and started to stand, as she did, her foot slid from under her pitching her toward the edge and death.

Vella made a strange gurgling sound as her head jerked back and then her shoulders and her back became curved like a bow. Pendal had her by the back of her jacket and was pulling her away from a fatal fall, the front of the jacket being closed was cutting across Vella's throat. Vella fell backwards on to her ass and looked up at Pendal who was still standing, unmoving with the reins of her horse in one hand as the other let go of Vella's jacket. "How strong are you?" She asked.

"Strong enough" responded Pendal and she again helped Vella to her feet. As Vella stood she ran her hand across Pendal's forearm and then her upper arm, "Body armour, I have never felt something so fine." She said. Then Vella caught sight of the soldiers on the other side, "They are with you, I take it?" She asked.

Pendal nodded, "I have come to take you and everyone North, where you will all be safe. Where is the NighT Guardian?" She asked.

Vella was more certain and more in control of herself now. "He is at the house with Cavahn. I came to tell them what happened to K'ola. Be gentle with him when you meet. When the Emperor emptied the prison, he said he had no use for any of the older guardians. The NighT Guardian was pensioned off and his privileges removed." Vella paused before continuing, "He has been sitting out on the verandah with nothing to do except the things Cavahn asks of him. He is lost, he is without purpose." Said Vella quietly as if their father could hear her speak.

A Homecoming

Pendal tied the reins of her horse to the post by the family shower. There was cool clear liquid in a small trough fed from the liquid that filled the shower, Pendal had never been able to explain why it was there, now she saw that it was for her horse, on this night. She put grains for him to eat in a bowl also attached there, for this night so long ago.

The NighT Guardian sat with his back to her, he was sleeping, arms resting on the chair arms and his chin on his chest, she could hear the snores of a man now without purpose in his life, he was dreaming of adventures from a younger age. Cavahn appeared at the door and looked over at the NighT Guardian, her face a mixture of resignation, concern and doubt. Then she turned to look at Pendal and her expression changed.

Pendal made a sign that indicated silence.

Vella stood beside Pendal; she looked and still was, a mess in all respects, physically, emotionally, and she was starting to smell from the animal feces on the trail she had been kneeling and sitting on. Vella was at the edge of a cliff, and still looking over at the huge pool of grief that she was about to plunge into and in which she could not swim.

Cavahn understood the need for silence and simply pointed at Vella and the shower, like a young child, Vella obeyed.

Pendal walked past Cavahn and stood behind the NighT Guardian. He did not wake and Pendal knew then that his reflexes and senses had deserted him. When duty and obligation are stripped away the things that allowed a person to be this or that role are not needed and shed. He was no longer a guardian and did not need the reflexes he had once prized. But he was her father and she would not allow him to continue like this.

She placed her strong slender hands on his shoulders and squeezed.

The NighT Guardian's chin came up off his chest sharply and he tried to turn his head to see who it was. But Pendal moved her hands to the base of his neck and started to massage the tension away that she found there. She moved her hands up the side of his neck and into the base of the skull and then around the cheeks and his jaw. She moved her hands back down and into the deeper muscles between his shoulder blades.

He moved his right hand up and held hers, stopping the massage, "That is enough, thank you. I knew you would return." As he spoke he turned in his seat to look at Pendal. "I did not know you would find an old man not a Guardian of the NighT."

Pendal squeezed his hand and stepped back. "Get up!" She said sternly, "Now! Get up! We are leaving." She looked into the NighT Guardian's eyes, they were slow to move and his face was slow to register her instructions.

She pushed out her foot and found the leg of the chair and pushed hard and the chair switched around a quarter turn almost tipping the NighT Guardian out of it. "Now! Get up! We are leaving." She repeated.

The NighT Guardian sat looking at her, his head moved as he scanned her from head to foot and foot to head. Then he nodded and placed a hand on the table to help him get out of his chair. As he stood he looked in to her eyes yes he seemed to be saying it was time to leave and he turned and shuffled towards the door, there was no energy in his movements. Suddenly all the scars and battles and tests he had put his body through had accumulated and drained him and wore him down. In her mind, Pendal started forming a plan for him.

As the NighT Guardian arrived at the front door, Cavahn appeared, she carried a backpack over each shoulder and one in her hand. Also, thrown over a shoulder were clothes for Vella who now stood in a drying cloth a few paces from her mother. Cavahn simply dropped a backpack at Vella's feet and the clothes on top of the pack.

Vella studied them without moving.

Cavahn dropped a pack in front of the NighT Guardian who stopped his shuffling motion toward the door, as he looked at the pack, Cavahn reached back inside the front door and took his cloak, staff and boots and threw them on the verandah floor beside the pack. Then she took Vella's boots and her own and placed them on the verandah floor and reached back, closed the door, locked it and set the projection shield to maximum, then it snapped into place. She looked at the NighT Guardian, "The upstairs is already closed and shielded."

She stepped forward and placed her feet in her boots and pulled a cloak around her. Slowly, the NighT Guardian put on his boots and in silence Vella dressed and put on her boots.

One by one, single file, they followed Pendal and her horse back up to the trail Pendal and Vella knew so well.

Pendal was surprised.

They were making good time. They were just past the last place she had last rested when they stopped. The journey seemed to have energized The NighT Guardian. It was not so much the walking and exercise but the idea that he was doing something secret that needed silence and strict mental discipline. Foot placement so that tracking was not easy and being careful not to leave broken branches and twigs. Even Pendal's horse seemed to be trained for this effort and left little trail of its own.

To make the journey easier, they had all placed their packs on Pendal's horse. When they slept the first time Pendal took a location separate from the others. It gave her a chance to communicate with one of the officers and provide information on who was now journeying north. The decision to leave quickly had been Pendal's but she had not expected Cavahn to have already prepared for it by having their packs ready.

Cavahn had explained she packed them shortly after Pendal had left that first evening when her bloodline became known to the family. She knew Pendal would return, but not when. Cavahn had also preyed that Pendal would come to take them away from the life they had started to lead, the retirement of the NighT Guardian had been as shocking and disruptive to Cavahn and Vella as it had been to the man himself.

While Cavahn had known that Pendal would return she had not expected to find the woman she walked beside. Pendal seemed taller and more lithe and powerful, she was self-assured, assertive and decisive, most important she had come to terms with her life at the Garfan monastery and had turned it into a powerful support and resource for her being. Cavahn had not foreseen that Garfan would elevate Pendal to a Demis Priest but she found it acceptable and has proud of her. As others had pointed out, Pendal was out in the world, not cloistered away in a monastery as tradition said, rather Pendal was a fighter and by all that Cavahn had heard, Pendal was now a brutally efficient one not afraid to kill. That made her something different, it made her a Den-kar Priest and she showed Pendal how rearranging the sacred symbols on her cuffs would make that declaration possible.

Pendal had simply replied that she did not feel she was a Demis Priest let alone this new type of priest Cavahn was telling her she was. Cavahn had become abrupt and simply told her that her life's purpose was defined before her spirit entered the physical body it now inhabited. She had no choice in the matter. She told Pendal that to decide to be known, as a Den-kar Priest was something she alone could resolve to be, it was not a rank gifted or bestowed by anyone.

Silence walked with them until the next Morning Rise.

The NighT Guardian had memories appropriate to the occasion, his mind wandered through past times when had been marching to the Legion banner, going to places where the Emperor required him to be, and he had to be ready to fight when he arrived. He came to relish the occasional glimpses of the VodaKhan troops guarding them and his mind would wander to those times when the Legion banner did not fly high at the front of a column but was hidden away so that the force could move quietly and without being seen.

Pendal rose before Morning Rise to mediate and clear her mind and ground herself with her guardian spirits, she needed the time more on the way back than on the journey to bring her family home. She had never before experienced the need for others to be safe and protected; she had never been concerned and worried for others, this was new to her. A voice told her that morning that a part of her was coming out of a shell that had been closed for far too long. It told her she needed this feeling.

She focused also on the trail.

The work to carve a way through the increasingly rocky terrain on the northern section had not been as elaborate as the main route down by the river. Often the steps and ledges made by the stone workers who cut through the rock outcroppings were still there rather than being made smooth. And the route through the outcroppings was often just wide enough to pass through. On the way down she had waited for her guards to pass through ahead of her, there was danger going south and out of VodaKhan, not so much going in the other direction.

First Sun was still low in the morning sky, bright and glowing as they came to a narrow gap cut through a steep rock outcropping. The route turned hard right after passing through the gap and descended into a small valley that emptied a small violent river into the broader one down by the main route. Beside the trail, tall always-green trees stood guard protecting the animals of the wood and the remains of trees cut down long ago that were rotting into the ground. They made a barrier to anyone trying to leave the narrow route.

Voices could be heard from the other side of gap in the rock outcropping. The source of the voices could not be seen, but they were coming closer and the plodding sound of their horses was clear and distinct.

Pendal looked at The NighT Guardian and then at Cavahn and Vella. With the trees so close on either side and the rotting remains of trees on the ground and in the bushes there was no where to get off the route to make way for the other riders, but a voice said to

Pendal to prepare herself, the riders were not merchants or farmers.

Three horsemen

Appeared.

They stopped and looked at Pendal's small party ahead of them, a small party that was blocking them.

The first two were Imperial soldiers complete with battle shields and long blades; they wore tunics stained with dried blood. The third behind them wore a tunic clean of any death or destruction. He was not a soldier.

Pendal looked at her shadow on the ground soil and saw that it was taller than she was and it stretched straight out from her feet, it was not angled from one side or to the other. The first sun of Day Rise was directly at her back and in their eyes.

She saw the shadow of the Night Guardian edging toward her, and in the moment he reached out to touch her she started to run towards the horsemen. Straight toward the horsemen she was using the bright glare of First Sun to hide her as much as it could.

As she ran, she reached over her right shoulder and took out her long blade. To one side of the lead horseman there still existed steps and a small work ledge left behind by the stone workers who had cut this gap.

At the last moment Pendal crossed the route path and the horseman on that side, he spotted her. He slipped his left hand into the fastening of his shield, a shield with long spikes intended to be thrust into an opponents face and chest. But in his haste one of the long spikes caught on some loose leather on his saddle. He struggled to bring the shield up to face Pendal, as he struggled with the shield his body blocked his hand from drawing his long blade.

Pendal leapt easily from the ground soil to the bottom rock step then to the second and on to the work ledge and from there she leapt at the horseman, as she was in the air she performed an aerial twist that placed her foot at the base of a row of shield spikes pushing it down and away from her. This movement of the shield caused the rider's hand to became entangled in the complex straps at the back of the shield. His hand and body was forced to follow the shield down and away exposing the back of his neck which Pendal sliced open with a swing of her long blade.

Placing one foot on the broad stiff saddle plate at the back of the now dead rider she sprang to a work ledge on the other side of the route. The second horseman looked at her face to face in a mix of shock which changed to a frenzied desire to kill her. In the moment it took him to display these emotions Pendal's short blade came from its sheath at her back and was driven up through his chin into his skull.

Pendal stepped past him on to the broad stiff saddle plate and jumped down taking several fast steps as she landed towards the third horseman who was trying to both turn his horse and back up all at the same time.

Her long blade slashed through the morning air and cut the reins just under the horse's mouth without touching the animal. The rider now had no control over the horse except with his feet, which he dug hard into the animal's side causing it to scream loudly. She ducked under the horse's head and came out swinging the butt end of her long blade at the riders exposed, unarmored thigh just above the knee.

The butt end carried a heavy weight to balance the long blade so perfectly for her. Pendal leapt up into the air and twirled to add her body weight to the twist and brought the butt end crashing on to the rider's leg above the knee breaking all the bones in the thigh and creating an enormous scream from the rider.

Pendal's movement allowed her to land on some steps still in the rock wall. She now looked at the rider, eye to eye. She became aware of the animals of the forest and the sky had gone silent, the riders scream of pain was that of an animal severely hurt and possibly about to die.

She fixed her gaze on the rider, he had thrown away the animal skin reins and was desperately trying to hold his shattered leg and stop the horse's movements, the movements brought intense agony as the shattered bones jarred against each other.

Perhaps she thought, this one does not need to die, yet!

She stepped out into mid air and with her left hand grasped the collar of his tunic at the back of his neck and let her body weight pull him from his saddle. He screamed loudly and violently as he hit the ground with his crushed leg twisted horribly.

The NighT Guardian, Cavahn, and Vella stood motionless. The NighT Guardian closed his mouth, he had not seen a person so lithe and acrobatic and yet totally deadly in action before. He had never seen anyone attack two mounted Imperial guards from on foot and use the terrain and its features so completely and effectively. Pendal steadied the third rider's horse and then started to bring all the horses through the narrow rock cut.

As she handed the reins of the two horses to the NighT Guardian VodaKhan guards surrounded them with more rushing past them to the rock gap and making sure the two fallen guards were dead, they also poured through the gap to make sure there were no more Imperial guards on the other side.

There were no more Imperial guards, or guards of any sort.

The Guard Captain came sliding down the rocky slope behind the gap and tried to jump the last few steps but missed and was pitched forward as his foot caught the step awkwardly causing him to almost fall flat on his face as he landed.

As he arrived in front of Pendal she was cleaning blood from her long blade using grasses and a leaf she knew was good for such things. A soldier passed him Pendal's hand blade and he now presented it to her as if he were presenting delicacies on a platter at a grand reception.

His apologies were many and complex.

Pendal waved them aside as she watched a soldier putting new reins on the horse without any. "We now have horses for all of my family. Search the saddlebags for any explanation of who these people are. I especially want to know where the dried blood on their tunics came from." The officer nodded and turned sharply to give orders and take the third rider who was writhing on the ground into custody.

Return to Pletke

Third sun was low in the sky.

The harsh smell of burned crops, and death.

But not the village, it was to the south of the village. Pendal's now openly well-guarded group came to a stop at the first of several rings of VodaKhan guards, they were directing them around the scene of a battle. Crops and plantings had been set on fire and there were many dead, mostly as far as Pendal could determine, Imperial Guards.

The NighT Guardian brought his horse next to Pendal's but remained silent as he surveyed the scene. This was all too familiar for him and he had thought he would not see it again, this was unwelcome and brought back memories of fallen friends and injuries he had sustained.

A VodaKhan officer rode up and provided a briefing, "The imperial party came from the south, they took the main route, and not the one you used. They surprised and destroyed a small outer encampment, but that group of brave men managed to stall the Imperials and raise the alarm. The fight was here," he waved his arm in the direction of the burned fields and bodies. "We saw three escape, they were headed in the direction of the old route, the one you were taking."

"Both Imperial Guards are dead," said Pendal in a blunt matter of fact tone. "We have the third, he does not look like an officer, or even military." She indicated over her shoulder at a litter on which lay the third horseman.

The officer looked over at the figure lying in pain on the litter, which had been set on the ground. "Why is he in pain and on a litter, he does not look like he is wounded?" Asked the officer.

"I shattered his leg!" Said Pendal.

The officer continued to stare at the body on the litter, "I assume we will have more stories to tell of your exploits. Oskar will want him," He said pointing at the litter. Then he waved over a soldier who would take them to Oskar.

Oskar sat at the large conference table listening to the officer who accompanied Pendal report. Oskar was clearly displeased at the revelations of what had happened in the rock gap and he said so. But, it again reaffirmed his faith in Pendal's ability to seize the initiative and be victorious.

As Pendal approached with her family, Oskar waved the officer away and rose from his seat. As was tradition when a group of family members meet someone of rank and importance they formed a loose circle, Pendal to the right of Oskar, then Cavahn and Vella, on Oskar's left The NighT Guardian.

Introductions were simple and factual. They were not about rank, but what the person speaking was skilled at. Vella induced herself as a healer, Cavahn as a priest, the NighT Guardian as an old soldier with knowledge of things military.

Cavahn then offered to be with the soldiers who required observance of their spirit crossing over as their physical form passed into lifelessness. Vella offered her skills as a healer to add to those already caring for and healing injured soldiers. Both offers were gratefully accepted and guides provided to take them to where in the camp their skills were needed.

Oskar turned to The NighT Guardian and held his arm and looked him in the eye for several moments, "We need you, we need you a lot. I hope like your daughter, we will be friends," said Oskar.

The NighT Guardian looked at Pendal and back at Oskar "we will be friends," he said simply. Then he reached out and held Oskar's arm and they hugged. "Please, if you can," said the NighT Guardian. "Tell us what happened here?"

A round table stood at the end of the large conference table; usually it would be used to carry refreshments for those at the bigger table but Oskar, Pendal and the NighT Guardian pulled chairs close to it as Oskar laid out a map of Pletke and its surroundings. A red shaded area indicated where the battle had commenced.

Oskar stabbed the shaded area with a paper knife, "less than half a cohort of heavily armed Imperial Guards and that rather interesting person Pendal captured, came across the border in the direction of Pletke. They surprised a light guard formation that fought well and allowed us to rally our forces on the northern side of the village. The offensive was divided in two; a force came around each side of the village taking the Imperials by surprise and making them fight on two sides and with the force in front of them which we managed to reinforce by coming through the village." Oskar paused and looked at the NighT Guardian as if asking for approval or comment but there was nothing the NighT Guardian offered other than a strong nod to what had been said.

"The rest is battle!" Exclaimed Oskar. "Blood, broken bones and death. The Imperials did not seem to want to surrender, and they did not want to turn around and leave either," said Oskar breathing slowly.

The NighT Guardian studied the map for a moment and then looked at Oskar, "the tunics are from the twelfth legion, a so-so legion, not bad, not good, their numbers are used to add weight not finesse to a battle. Yet the fight you describe they put up and the level of equipment I have seen tells me they are from a much stronger unit accustomed to first order battle. Finding out which will help assess the importance of what they might have been looking for. Also, the force is meager, I believe it was here to find something and take it south. When they decided to hold fast they did not realize how substantial the force was they were fighting. They had no spies and no intelligence."

Oskar nodded at the assessment. "But why come across fields of plantings when staying on the route would have been easier?" He asked for help with this question.

As NighT Guardian studied the map, Pendal looked troubled, "Why did we not see them on the route?" Then she answered her own question, "I know, we were in the rock cuttings and woods for most of the last part of the journey." She seemed genuinely troubled that the group she was leading did not detect the Imperial forces.

The Night Guardian indicated on the map a route that ran along beside the river on the far side and a similar old route higher up and probably like the one they took, hidden from view. He then turned his attention back to the where the Imperial party had suddenly cut across fields of dense plantings which had slowed their progress and made their retreat more difficult. "All I can think of is time. They were behind schedule or maybe a forward scout had spotted your forces down near the route and they decided cutting across the fields made sense," he indicated with his hand on the map, "it would be quicker and easier when they had trampled the plantings." He looked thoughtful, "but perhaps what they were looking for was located in this part of the village," he picked up a measuring stick and placed it on the map, "from where they left the route, they rode in a straight line, that line would take them to this part of the village. What is there here?" He asked pointing to the map.

The map was not detailed enough to show buildings just the important features such as the village boundary, and the fountain where Pendal had judged the Grey Priest. Oskar stared at the map without saying anything his mind was a blank.

"The harvester's building is at that end of the village, it is the only large structure," said Pendal looking at Oskar and then the NighT Guardian. "We missed something when we were last there," she said.

Oskar looked at her in surprise, and nodded vigorously.

The Harvester's House

Pendal pulled out a chair and sat down.

To one side of her, also sitting was Oskar, on the other side the NighT Guardian.

They sat in silence, taking in the main hall, the height of the rafters, the length of the room, the windows which were partially shaded to keep out the brightness of full Day Rise. They studied the arrangement of the sleeping areas, and they looked at the floor. They had listened to the sound of their boots on the floor as they entered. They were stretching their awareness to let the building tell them what was out of place and might conceal what the Imperials had come to retrieve.

Then each at their own discretion slowly started to move around the space, Oskar and the NighT Guardian were walking in step and talking quietly, that pleased Pendal. The NighT Guardian seemed energized again; he had a purpose and was connected again to things military. It was possible the plan Pendal had hatched in her mind back on the verandah would work.

Pendal found herself at the showers and toilet facilities. The harvesters had bathed before they left for the fields. A window high in the wall had not been shaded as well as those in the main hall making this area brighter than the space outside, the trails of river liquid from the shower stalls led to a series of large central drains and the wetness could still be seen on the floor.

Trails led to all drains except one. To the far one, there were no liquid trails. Pendal stood focusing on the drain, the shower stalls and the other trails which she could clearly see. As she breathed in and let the space talk to her, she felt Oskar and the NighT Guardian join her. As she felt their presence, she reached behind her and took out her long blade. She walked slowly into the shower area and studied the pristine, dry, drain cover. She squatted and placed her long blade over it. The tip nodded up and down no matter which way she turned the blade. The drain cover was dry because it was slightly higher than the floor though by trickery of woodwork the drain appeared to be the same height as the rest.

"We need some men," said Oskar, "to raise the drain."

Raising the drain proved to be quite easy, the grate over the top had been formed to look complex, like the others, but in fact was an easy handhold, and after a little resistance, it lifted cleanly upwards with a section of the floor. Once out of the way the entrance to a tunnel was revealed.

Oskar would flatly not allow Pendal or the NighT Guardian to go into the tunnel; instead he sent two pairs of soldiers with a short time distance between them. This allowed the first pair to explore and if they got into trouble the second pair could act as rescuers, but more important, they were to report back on what they found.

It did not take long.

All four soldiers came out of the tunnel with information that it appeared to go under the laneway, at the end they found steps leading up to a cover. Carefully lifting it they did indeed find themselves in the basement of the building across the laneway. The room was full of crates and other covered items which they did not disturb. As far as they could hear, the building was not occupied.

Oskar dispatched soldiers to encircle the building and the NighT Guardian suggested doing the same to the ones on either side. Guards were placed inside the Harvesters building and at the entrance, it was also encircled.

As Pendal came out into full Day Raise she shaded her eyes at the brightness but in the Northern lands there was not the need for the heavy cloaks worn in the south, something the NighT Guardian happily commented on. Before they tried to enter the house, they walked around the building noting any oddities that might increase their risk. Unlike the Harvester's building, this one had a garden of plantings and a small enclosure where tools were stored. They cautiously made their way around the plantings which to Pendal's eyes were in poor condition. At the enclosure Pendal picked up a cask of river liquid and splashed the contents on the floor. The liquid remained where she spilled it except in one corner where it ran between the wood floor beams.

While they waited for additional soldiers to come, the NighT Guardian went to move some bags of ground soil nutrient but instead of the expected weight he found the bags were stuffed with dry plantings and were only made to look heavy and difficult to move. By the time the extra soldiers appeared, he had found the handle that allowed him to pull up a section of floor with little effort.

Oskar gave the same instructions as he had to the soldiers who searched the tunnel in the Harvester's building. The response after a few moments was the same; they came to steps leading up to a cover in the floor of the house.

As Oskar, Pendal and the NighT Guardian stood looking up at the house, Pendal reached back and took out her long blade.

"Pendal, you are not to enter," it was the NighT Guardian speaking not Oskar. "There could be traps and hidden weapons that could kill and maim and you would not see them until too late," he said. He turned to look at Oskar who was watching this father daughter interaction. "Oskar my friend, I should lead as I have extensive knowledge of such things. If they are indeed there I could help to save the soldiers, but Pendal is not to enter on any account," he said calmly but forcefully.

Oskar turned and held out an arm in the direction of the building, "Please, my friend, lead on."

As they walked toward the building Pendal put away her long blade and Oskar started issuing orders that men should follow and take orders from the NighT Guardian. As she watched Oskar and her father make the final decisions a smile briefly spread across her face, the use of "friend," and "my friend" seemed to be natural and unforced, this is what Pendal had hoped would happen, what she asked her guiding spirits to help create, but how what she asked for would come to pass, she had no idea. Now she was seeing it unfold.

No one was found in the building. There was plenty of evidence of it being used as a make shift armory, there were sufficient weapons found to equip half of a cohort, but there was also gold, at the lowest level, where the tunnels came up through the floor the boxes, crates and covered piles where filled with a ransom of gold. Oskar estimated it was the equivalent of what they would load on a ship at one of the Northern ports before it headed south. But, as he examined markings on the strips of gold, he could also say they were not from recent shipments and not all from one shipment, these had been accumulated over several cycles.

The house was also entrapped, there were many, all designed to maim and kill and required the NighT Guardian to make them safe before proceeding anywhere in the house. The upper level had been fortified as a holdout should the building be discovered and attacked and the escape tunnel to the garden could not be used.

Perhaps more interesting they found evidence the Emperor came here and staid for some time, as there were many changes of clothing, wildly expensive and ornate time keepers hanging on the wall in all the upstairs rooms, even one of gold; official clothing, and clothing in several legion colours. There was also plain clothing that would allow the Emperor, if he wished to look like an ordinary person to leave and walk or ride in ordinary Day Rise.

Most especially interesting they found two versions of the execution order for Sovan complete with Imperial seals attached. Neither version matched the one that was proclaimed at his finding of guilt. There were numerous other proclamations both finished and never issued or in draft form. And there were plans, many plans for seizing and controlling VodaKhan and how to dispose of the leadership. Those in the VodaKhan senate were also marked for execution; there was even a Senate roll call from a recent session to provide a detailed list of names of those to be executed.

While there was a lot of detail on how to remove the entire upper level of government and any possible threat, there was even more on how the Imperial forces would pillage and remove as much gold as they could during the first cycle they were in control and estimates by the Emperor on how much they could force from the mines in each of the next five cycles.

Transporting their spoils was documented but only very crudely, clearly the emperor was more interested in acquiring gold, and killing anyone who might be an obstruction than the bothersome detail of moving his spoils.

If there was resistance, he planned to stop food shipments from the south, and let the population starve during the long winter or until they gave in, or as he put it, "starvation will reduce and weaken the population, but if we can get it the point of human eating, human, the southern regions will look down on VodaKhan and we can kill as many as we want without any objection. We only really need enough alive to mine the gold"

Oskar, the NighT Guardian and Pendal read this and the rest of the documents in the safety of camp under the failing light of the last sun as messengers were sent to the capital with the most sensitive and damming of the papers.

Pendal reached for a small bowl attached to a cask of river liquid and dipped it in. Normally, the liquid would be used for cleaning hands before dinning "I feel as if I need to clean my hands after touching the papers," she said as she let the liquid run off her slender hands and on to the ground and not into the collection bowl. "I don't want any of this liquid to be collected and used again somewhere," she said in explanation as the others watched her.

Oskar nodded in agreement. The NighT Guardian threw the paper he was reading back on the pile and sat back in his chair, "All those years fighting and watching friends die for that turd…." His voice trailed off.

Jankor Van

Pendal sat on a table idly kicking her feet back and forth, Oskar sat on a simple military issue chair made of wood and cloth next to a cot that was made in similar fashion. The NighT Guardian stood to the right of Oskar looking down at the cot.

On the cot lay the survivor of Pendal's engagement at the rock cut, his smashed leg had been set with braces and some surgery had secured the bones. He was secured to the cot, which had been secured to the ground soil and would not move. Rivers of sweat ran down a face that was contorted with open lips, clenched teeth, and eyes that were tightly closed as if in brutal grief. Snot ran from his nose down his cheeks and was almost at his ears, breathing was a rapid series of harsh sounds as he inhaled and exhaled in massive gulps.

Oskar waved the healer to give more of the herbs used to extract information. The healer took a damp rag from a sealed jar and rubbed it over the man's teeth and held it against his nose. Breathing through the mouth or nose, he would get the full force of the herbs. Then the cloth was gone and back in the jar, and the jar sealed again.

There was silence for a moment as the man on the cot tried not to breath and take in more of the herbs but finally he gasped for air, and expelled a large ball of mucus on to his chest which heaved to take in air.

"Jankor Van, my name is Jankor Van" the man finally hissed.

Oskar looked around at Pendal who looked back and simply shrugged, she did not speak but her actions said the name was unfamiliar.

As Oskar turned to look at The NighT Guardian, the NighT Guardian spoke, "Shit!" He exclaimed.

"Why shit?" Oskar asked.

"The head of the imperial Army is Delon Cass. He is from a major house which married into the Imperial blood line many hundred cycles ago, but it in the legions this one," the NighT Guardian pointed to the man in the cot "was known to be the one that led the army, Delon Cass was just a mouth piece speaking what Jankor Van decided." He paused as he looked back and forth between Pendal and Oskar, "Jankor Van also did work for the Emperor that the Emperor would not trust to anyone else, and that included murder and torture" said the NighT Guardian. May I ask…." He looked at Oskar who was already nodding approval that the NighT Guardian could join the questioning.

"Which supply legion is coming north?" He asked.

Jankor Van hissed through his clenched teeth as he tried to use them to hold back the words the herbs were compelling him to speak but finally his mouth opened, "Seventeenth" was his answer.

"Who are they supporting?" Asked the NighT Guardian.

Again, Jankor Van hissed through his teeth but this time he also shook his head violently from side to side. The NighT Guardian moved closer to the man in the cot and knelt down by the mans head and whispered in his ear as he repeated his question.

"Second! They support the Second." Jankor Van growled as the words came out.

"Who else?" Asked the NighT Guardian.

The NighT Guardian looked up at Oskar, "The Seventeenth supply legion is capable of keeping more than one legion in the field at the same time."

Oskar nodded at the validity of how questioning was proceeding.

As they turned back to Jankor Van another ball of mucus was heaved on to his chest. "The Second, they support the Second and what the remains of the Black Legion."

"How much remains of the Black Legion?" Asked the NighT Guardian.

They all looked at Jankor Van with new intensity, the herbs had full control of his mind and his voice now; there was a certain peace to the man's expression and he was no longer clenching his teeth. Questioning would be much easier.

"Five cohorts of the original soldiers." He said rather peacefully and clearly.

"Why the Second?" Asked the Night Guardian.

"They plod but are complete and difficult to dislodge. They and the seventeenth draw the enemy as the remnants of the Black Legion strike for the mines." Jankor Van heaved a deep breath and seemed to relax as if a great weight of secrecy had finally been lifted from his shoulders.

Oskar leaned forward, "When will this happen?" He asked urgently.

"Before the first snow." Said Jankor Van easily and confidently.

"What is the gold in the village for?" Asked Pendal looking over the heads of the The NighT Guardian and Oskar.

Jankor Van seemed to hesitate causing Oskar to look at the healer who was administering the herbs but the healer indicated that no more were required. They waited in silence.

"The gold is for House Delar and the River Navigators Guild." He said finally.

Oskar rocked back on his chair a look of surprise on his face. But it was Pendal the continued questioning. "What does House Delar do for their share?" She asked.

Jankor Van started to breathe heavily and a look of strain appeared on his face, he was resisting the herbs. Oskar waved the healer to administer more and very quickly Jankor Van's face disappeared under a strong smelling grey cloth. Then the cloth was removed and Jankor Van's face had a tranquil expression and his voice was steady again and the answers came quickly.

"House Delar will create an Electoral Division in the VodaKhan senate. Our agents will set off explosives and use their weapons to kill as many of the senate as they can during the Division, the Emperor decided it would be easier than trying to round up the House leaders from their estates." He breathed heavily but started to relax his head and neck on the pillow.

"And, what will River Navigators Guild do for their share?" Questioned Pendal.

Jankor Van suddenly tried to test the restraints and surprised all of them, making them sit up or stand back; then he stopped and relaxed again.

"The Guild, will transport the Second Legion by river past the regular defenses, they have also shared the location of the southern most mines from which they transport gold by river today." Jankor Van looked exhausted and the healer requested they allow him to recover a normal mental state before continuing anymore questioning.

Messengers

Oskar finished the last if his messages and gave it to the soldier. He had written four messages, all given to soldiers with instructions to ride to capital and the High Protector by a different route. One soldier was sent on his own, he was the last Oskar had given a message to. This soldier would travel alone and not in uniform. The other messengers traveled with different levels of protection, one even had half a cohort with him. None were to stop, not even for rest and were to eat on horseback, Oskar demanded that they always be moving froward towards the capital no matter what happened.

Oskar looked at Pendal and the NigHT Guardian. "The Electoral Division House Delar is to create in the senate will require all the Leaders of each house to be preset, killing even a few of them would disrupt the VodaKhan government. But it is the River Navigators Guild that is very troubling." Oskar shook his head as he talked about the Guild. Then he picked up a writing instrument and paper and started another message. He was silent while he was writing.

As he finished, Oskar called for another messenger. The tunic this messenger wore was a dull silver with white markings of rank. The tunic was nothing like the ones worn by the other legions accompanying them.

After the messenger left Pendal looked Oskar in the eye, "What are you scheming, that is one of the soldiers you brought with you from the west, where we first met." She said.

Oskar picked up a glass of clear river liquid, sipped from it, and looked at Pendal and then the NighT Guardian. "I am moving some of the legions under my direct control. Some will move closer to the ports where we ship the gold from and others will move closer to the central region, where the capital is. In the far north there are legions that rarely see green grass or ground soil without snow the height of a horse covering it. They will move closer to the mines in the north and positions directly north of the capital. What do think Guardian?" Oskar said looking at the NighT Guardian.

After a few moments the NighT Guardian picked up his glass and sipped from it as well, he held it out for Oskar to chink his glass against. Both men looked at each other and smiled.

Pendal looked at the two smiling people in front of her and clicked her heels together and said sternly, "What are you toasting?"

Her father looked at Pendal and smiled. "Jankor Van has set a good plan and one that could easily succeed if not discovered. But he is also known for deviousness and creating plans within plans. It is possible that he planned to be captured, in fact," said the Night Guardian, "he may have wanted to be captured so he can be questioned and give up a version of his plan." He paused for Pendal to indicate she was following along.

"I am sure the part about using explosives and weapons in the senate to kill as many of the House Leaders as he can is true, and some troops will go by Guild transport but as the Guild has already given up the location of the mines they are of little value to the Emperor now." The NighT Guardian fell silent looking down into his glass. "Most will travel conventionally and those going by Guild river transport will attack any VodaKhan legions trying to stop the advance, from behind." Then he looked over at Oskar. "What he doesn't know is Oskar's ability to move legions he has no intelligence about." Again the

NighT Guardian and Oskar clinked their glass together.

As they went back to sipping the cool liquid, they looked over and watched soldiers preparing to leave with a train eight of heavy carts that would be rolling out of Pletke with the gold. There would be no gold to pay off House Delar or the River Navigators Guild. As they watched the guard detail leave to accompany the heavy carts Oskar reflected that not paying the House or the Guild may also be part of the plan.

While they reflected on the value of end events at Pletke Pendal meditated for a moment about Callar and how his spirit had come back to communicate to her and how it had brought them here; for a moment she felt something warm sitting beside here as if he were there, rubbing shoulders with her and she thanked the warm feeling.
The moment must have been longer than Pendal knew because when she came back to being in the NOW, Vella and Cavahn had joined them accompanied by several soldiers who were there to break their part of camp and pack it for the journey north.

Cavahn was standing in front of Pendal, there had been more need of the services she and Vella offered and both looked exhausted. As Pendal's spirit returned to the world Cavahn spoke to her, "I need your help, there is an old man, he harvests the crops around the village, he is about to pass over, he said you promised to observe it. He says he will hold on to this world until you come."

Pendal nodded.

The Passing of a Harvester

Pendal looked at the other Harvesters as she entered and one by one they hugged her and she hugged them back in return, nothing was said as one harvester took hold of her slender right hand and another her slender left hand and led her to the sleeping space where the Harvester she met and blessed by the river that night when she first set eyes on Pletke lay sleeping.

As she entered his space Vella and Cavahn slipped in to one side and stood quietly. The entrance to the harvesters sleeping area was closed off by his friends who brought stools and chairs to stand on and look over the top of the old mans sleeping area.

Pendal took a three legged stool from the side of his space and sat down, as she did she slipped one of her slender hands into the man's half open left hand. She lifted and stroked the back of his hand. It was a hand gnarled by work, hard manual toil, cuts and abrasions had accumulated over the years of his life she could see that each of his fingers and thumb had been broken and roughly reset. The small finger did not open properly due to some injury to ligaments on the side of his hand but her slender fingers could fit through the space that remained to allow her to hold his hand properly.

"I knew you would come" the voice was still strong and clear but when Pendal looked into his eyes she knew he did not see her. That part of his being had already receded from the physical world.

"I would not leave without this time together" She said. As she finished the words she felt a connection with the old mans spirit. After so long toiling in the fields and the river it wanted to leave the world and go back to the a place where there was no physical burden to get out of the cot each day to get food or suffer the emptiness of a belly that had not eaten for days. His spirit was tired of managing the sharp scything implements as they swished back and forth cutting down the crops, and it longed for a time when it could be without the sadness for receiving little reward for the hard effort the body put in.

He spoke of the wishes that had not been granted and things that had not been achieved. As he spoke his voice became soft and Pendal leaned forward until her head was almost on the pillow beside him.

All the time she replied softly in a similar tone and level that no one other than he could hear or understand, her spirit mingled with his and prepared it to leave. She sensed that this spirit would not struggle with that final step from the physical world, but she would make sure, she would not allow this man's spirit to walk through the village and the platings unable to get back into the physical world and too scared to step over in to the next.

All around there was silence except for the gentle murmuring talk of Pendal and the Harvester. Slowly the words became less and the air became more energized and charged around Pendal, the cot and the old man. Some could sense it, Cavahn could see it. There was a vibrancy to the light around Pendal, it was clear and crisply white like the colour of Third Moon. The colour around the old man was more mellow, like the glow seen at a distance as Third Sun started to pass out of the sky, and befitting his end of life.

At some moment after they stopped speaking, Pendal's brilliant white light spread over the cot and the old man wrapping and holding his mellow light there for a moment before it slowly absorbed into her light. As Cavahn watched with her heightened senses she could feel the old man's spirit re-emerge from Pendal's energy as she continued to lead it to a brilliant waterfall of energy and light.

At the waterfall, Pendal broke the waterfall creating an opening. The old man's energy seemed to hesitate but it was still connected with Pendal and she brought it close, closer and then the man's energy suddenly shot across the gap and through the opening.

Pendal closed the opening.

As she opened her dark liquid eyes she sat up and slipped her fingers out of the harvester 's hand, she said a small blessing she had learned at the monastery and placed her hands on her knees to help her get up.

Cavahn 's face as she looked at Pendal was one of absolute intensity, surprise and awe. She held out her hand to help Pendal stand and steady her. Quietly she said, "You have been doing that since you were eleven cycles! I can only honour you."

"... Life at Monastery." Was all Pendal said. As Pendal left the sleeping space, she was hugged again, and again, and again.

Outside, Pendal looked up at First Moon, it was already a full quarter of its way across the sky. Pendal turned to Cavahn and Vella, "I always loose track of time when I observe a passing" then she turned abruptly and started to head to the village fountain where soldiers waited with their horses.